Frederick Tennyson

**Poems of the Day and Year**

Frederick Tennyson

**Poems of the Day and Year**

ISBN/EAN: 9783337408558

Printed in Europe, USA, Canada, Australia, Japan

Cover: Foto ©Andreas Hilbeck / pixelio.de

More available books at **www.hansebooks.com**

# Poems of the Day and Year

TO
MY SON AND DAUGHTER
JULIUS AND SOPHIA TENNYSON
THE COMPANIONS OF
· MY OLD AGE

# CONTENTS

|  | PAGE |
|---|---|
| The Birth of the Year, | 1 |
| The Redbreast, | 6 |
| The First of March, | 9 |
| Hope, | 14 |
| April, | 20 |
| The Skylark and the Poet, | 25 |
| The Thirty-first of May, | 30 |
| The Cloud, | 36 |
| Noon, | 39 |
| To the Cicala, | 42 |
| To a Summer Fly, | 49 |
| The Forest, | 55 |
| The Fountain, | 61 |
| SONNETS— | |
| The Poet and the Fount of Happiness, | 64 |
| To Poesy, | 65 |
| The Prospect of evil days, | 66 |

# CONTENTS

|  |  | PAGE |
|---|---|---|
| The Blackbird, | . . . . . | 67 |
| The Poet to a caged Nightingale, | . . . | 74 |
| The glory of Nature, | . . . . | 83 |
| The Mountains, | . . . . | 86 |
| The Temple, | . . . . . | 91 |
| The Golden City, | . . . . | 97 |
| To the Poet, | . . . . . | 104 |
| Death and the Shepherd, | . . . | 108 |
| Follow Now, | . . . . . | 113 |
| Women and Children, | . . . . | 126 |
| The Coming Day, | . . . . | 130 |
| Harvest Home, | . . . . | 134 |
| The Eleventh of September, | . . . | 140 |
| The Flight of the Swallow, | . . . | 143 |
| Evening, | . . . . . | 147 |
| The Garlands of Memory, | . . . | 152 |
| The Holytide, | . . . . | 156 |

# THE BIRTH OF THE YEAR

LET us speak low; the infant is asleep :

  The frosty hills grow sharp, the day is near,

And Phosphor with his taper comes to peep

  Into the cradle of the new-born year ;

    Hush ! the infant is asleep,

      Monarch of the day and night;

      Whisper—yet it is not light—

    The infant is asleep.


Those arms shall crush great serpents; ere to-
morrow

  His closed eyes shall wake to laugh and weep;

His lips shall curl with mirth, and writhe with
sorrow,

A

And charm up truth and beauty from the deep:
　　Softly, softly let us keep
　　　Our vigils ; visions cross his rest ;
　　　Prophetic pulses stir his breast,
　　Altho' he is asleep.

Now Love and Death armed in his presence
　　wait,
　　Genii with lamps are standing at the door;
Oh ! he shall sing sweet songs, he shall relate
　　Wonder, and glory, hopes untold before :
　　　Murmur memories, that may creep
　　　　Into his ears, of eld sublime:
　　　　Let the youngest-born of Time
　　　Hear music in his sleep.

Quickly he shall awake : the East is bright,
　　And the hot glow of the unrisen sun
Hath kissed his brow with promise of its light,
　　His cheek is red with victory to be won :

Quickly shall our King awake,

   Strong as giants, and arise;

   Sager than the old and wise

The infant shall awake.


His childhood shall be froward, wild, and thwart

   His gladness fitful, and his angers blind;

But tender spirits·shall o'ertake his heart,

   Sweet tears, and golden moments bland and

      kind.

   He shall give delight, and take,

     Charm, enchant, dismay, and soothe,

     Raise the dead, and touch with youth;

   Oh ! sing that he may wake !


Where is the sword to gird upon his thigh ?

   Where is his armour and his laurel crown ?

For he shall be a Conqueror ere he die,

   And win him kingdoms wider than his own :

Like the earthquake he shall shake
  Cities down, and waste like fire;
  Then build them stronger, pile them
    higher
When he shall awake.


In the dark spheres of his unclosed eyes
  The sheathed lightnings lie, and clouded stars,
That shall glance softly, as in summer skies,
  Or stream o'er thirsty deserts, winged with wars.
    For in the pauses of dread hours
      He shall fling his armour off,
      And like a reveller sing and laugh,
    And dance in ladies' bowers.


Ofttimes in his mid-summer he shall turn
  To look on the dead Spring with weeping eyes,
O'er ashes of pale Beauty stand and mourn,
  And kiss the bier of stricken Hope with sighs;

Ofttimes, like light of onward seas,

He shall hail great days to come,

Or hear the first dread note of doom,

Like torrents on the breeze.


His manhood shall be blissful and sublime

With stormy sorrows, and serenest pleasures;

And his crowned age upon the top of time

Shall throne him, great in glories, rich in
treasures;

The sun is up, the day is breaking;

Sing ye softly, draw anear;

Immortal be the new-born year,

And blessed be its waking !

# TO THE REDBREAST

REDBREAST, that fliest from the starved wood,
   Thy homeless misery scorning to complain,
That speaking eye is not to be withstood,
   Thy patience pleads not to my heart in vain;
The wind is whirling and the snows descend ;
Friend, come to me and I will be thy friend.

Lone bird, altho' thou hast no songs of joy
   To glad me when the nightingale's are dumb,
No golden plumage to enchant mine eye,
   Thou comest to me when no others come :
'Tis Hope that makes thee at my casement stand,
'Tis Faith that bids thee fly into my hand.

Thou lookest in my face with eyes of cheer
   That win me in affliction not to weep ;
A voice in thy mute sympathy I hear—
   ' Hope is not dead, tho' Joy is fallen asleep ' :
Ah ! would to Heaven that in my days of ill
My winged heart, like thine, were fearless still !

It saith, ' Tho' friends forsake thee, there is one,
   Tho' penury cling unto thee, do not fear ;
Tho' days be darkling, they must be outrun,
   And thou and I shall see another year ' :
Thou hast my heart, kind bird ; oh ! give me
      thine,
That I may neither sorrow nor repine !

It saith, ' When glories from the world depart,
   And youth is past, oh ! linger not alone ' :
It saith, ' When shadows thicken round thy heart
   Fly forth, and look on ills beyond thine own ;

And Age shall not behold his thin, grey hairs,

And Sorrow shall forget his daily cares.'

It saith, 'When days are burning to their end,

   And the mind flutters, and the limbs are chill,

There is an inner thought that cannot bend

   Before the dread reality of ill' :

Nature's great soul is shadowed forth in thee,

Life under ashes of mortality !

# FIRST OF MARCH

THROUGH the gaunt woods the winds are
    shrilling cold,
  Down from the rifted rack the sunbeam pours
  Over the cold grey slopes and stony moors;
The glimmering watercourse, the eastern wold,
And over it the whirling sail o' the mill,
  The lonely hamlet with its mossy spire,
  The piled city smoking like a pyre,
Fetched out of shadow, gleam with light as chill.

The young leaves pine, their early promise
    stayed;
  The hope-deluded sorrow at the sight

Of the sweet blossoms by the treacherous
  light
Flattered to death, like tender love betrayed ;
And step-dames frown, and aged virgins chide;
  Relentless hearts put on their iron mood;
  The hunter's dog lies dreaming of the wood,
And dozes barking by the ingle-side.


Larks twitter, martins glance, and curs from far
  Rage down the wind and straight are heard
    no more;
  Old wives peep out, and scold, and bang the
    door,
And clanging clocks grow angry in the air :
Sorrow and care, perplexity and pain,
  Frown darker shadows on the homeless one ;
  And the grey beggar buffeting alone
Pleads in the howling storm, and pleads in
  vain.

The field-fires smoke along the champaign drear,
 And drive before the north wind, streaming
  down
 Bleak hill, and furrow dark, and fallow brown;
Few living things along the land appear:
The weary horse looks out, his mane astray,
 With anxious fetlock, and uneasy eye,
 And sees the market carts go madly by
With sidelong drivers reckless of the way.

The sere beech-leaves that trembled dry and
  red
 All the long winter on the frosty bough,
 Or slept in quiet underneath the snow,
Fly off, like resurrections of the dead :
The horny ploughman and his yoked ox
 Wink at the icy blasts; and beldames old,
 Stout and red hooded, flee before the cold,
And children's eyes are blinded by the shocks.

You cannot hear the waters for the wind:

  The brook that foams, and falls, and bubbles
    by,

  Hath lost its voice—but ancient steeples sigh,

And belfries moan—and crazy ghosts, confined

In dark courts, weep, and shake the shuddering
    gates,

  And cry from points of windy pinnacles,

Howl thro' the bars, and plain among the
    bells,

And shriek, and wail like voices of the Fates!


And who is he that down the mountain side,

  Swift as a shadow flying from the sun,

  Between the wings of stormy winds doth run,

With fierce blue eyes and eyebrows knit with
    pride;

Tho' now and then I see sweet laughters play

  Upon his lips, like moments of bright heaven

Thrown 'twixt the cruel blasts of morn and
    even,
And golden locks beneath his hood of grey?


Sometimes he turns him back to wave farewell
    To his pale sire with icy beard and hair ;
    Sometimes he sends before him thro' the air
A cry of welcome down a sunny dell :
And while the echoes are around him ringing,
    Sudden the angry wind breathes low and
        sweet ;
    Young violets show their blue eyes at his feet,
And the wild lark is heard above him singing !

# HOPE

ANGELS of beauty are abroad to-day,
   And ministers of bliss; the winds are sleeping,
And thro' a thin-wove veil of silvery grey
   The sun is like a timid lover peeping,
Where Hope in her own garden stands and
      sings,
   And gazing upward hears the skylark chiming
Wild response to her song, and with his wings
   Sweet measure to his eager music chiming.

She sang, 'They say that I am false as fair,
   That these blue eyes are fickle, vain this
      breath,

Mine idle aims impalpable as air,

My life a lie, and all its triumphs death ;

For when I clutch the amaranth flower of Joy,

Wealth's golden urn, the laurels of the Muse,

Joy, Wealth, and Fame may live, but Hope

I die,

Like rainbows followed thro' their own sweet

dews.


' Thankless are they : who arms the heart of

youth ?

Who fires the lover's song, the hero's eye ?

Who breathes the hermit's prayer, the martyr's

truth ?

Who makes it bliss to live, and peace to die ?

Thankless are they, and heed not what they say;

There is no armour against ill but mine ;

When beauty, strength, and youth are fled away

The living light within mine eyes doth shine.

' These limbs can be a giant's in their might,

    This still, small voice a trumpet clear and
        loud,

These tearful orbs, that tremble in the light,

    Strong as an eagle's soaring through a cloud :

I raise the fond eyes and the listening ears

    Of babes to their first friend; I meet the frown

Of the last enemy full arm'd with fears;

    I give him battle and I cast him down.'


But while she spoke, a shadow o'er the plain

    Swept softly, and she turned, and there there
        lay

The wondrous arch built up of sun and rain,

    And dyed the far-off woods with hues of May :

She ran in haste to scale those steps of fire ;

    The weeping Iris, jealous of her eyes,

Drew then her ladder back, lest Hope aspire

    Earth-born to mount unbidden to the skies.

Where are the glories that she saw from
  far ?
There is no beauty, but the frown instead
Of angry winter armed again for war,
  Grim with blown mantle o'er the mountain
    head :
Her eyes were filled with tears, her heart beat
    fast ;
  The dewy drops shower'd round her as she
    came ;
Homeward she bent her jocund steps at last,
  And laughed with mirth the while she blushed
    with shame.


Lightly she stepped, and lo ! beyond the shade
  Of the grey storm, she saw the sunny lea,
Like an empyreal shore, that seemed to fade
  In the far azure ether like a sea;

B

And stream and lawn, steep wood, and templed
    town
  Flashed forth like isles of glory, and she sung—
‘ So do my blisses lie beyond the frown
  Of envious Time; my heart is ever young.’

She sang—‘ I'll take the eagle's wings, and scale
  The mighty walls that stand against the sky;
I'll take the crescent moon, and softly sail
  Upon the winding amber streams, that lie
Betwixt the clouds; I'll take a beam, and run
  Up to the diamond gates of Paradise;
I'll peep behind the curtains of the sun,
  And see the fountains of the day arise.’

Far o'er the woods into the midst of morn,
  Ceasing her song, she turned her straining
    sight,
And the pale mountains on their fronts forlorn

Caught her warm smile, and laughed with
  sudden light :
The sun flashed forth in answer to her smile,
  And filled the world with radiant ecstasies :
Then to her garden flowers she turned awhile,
  Pansies and violets like her own blue eyes.

# APRIL

April, April, child of Mirth
And Sorrow, sweetest face on earth !
Oh ! but to name thee fills my ears
With songs, mine eyes with pleasant tears ;
For so thou wert when I was young,
And called thee with a lisping tongue ;
So shalt thou be when I am old,
And loves and fears alike are cold.

Tho' others change, thou wilt not change ;
But alway something swift and strange,
Like shadows followed by the sun
From thee across my heart shall run ;

While the tender breath from thee
Sheds life o'er turf and forest tree,
Pours love-notes thro' the valleys lone,
And brings me back the swallow flown.

To pale, sad grief thy presence seems
A shape of light in mist of dreams.
Thou singest in the ears of Joy ;
He shakes his locks, th' enchanted boy ;
And the clouds soar up, and pile
The vast with silver hill and isle,
Or under golden arches run
Great rivers pouring from the sun.

Ofttimes I mark thee stepping thro'
The mist, thy fair hair strung with dew,
Or by the great stair of the dawn
Come down by river, croft, and lawn,
Thy sun—and cloud—inwoven vest
Rippling its skirts from east to west,

And glancing on the breeze and light,
Dash the wildflowers left and right.

Ofttimes in moments soft and fair
Under the clear and windless air
Thou sleepest, and thy breathings low
In blissful odours come and go ;
And oft in moments proud and wild
Thou spoilest, like a froward child,
The blossoms thou hast just laid on,
And laughest when the ill is done.

Again I see thee run and leap
From gusty peaks—or stand and weep
Tears, like Memory's, that distil
Hopes of good thro' days of ill ;
And the peaceful rainbow hides
The thunders on the mountain sides
With its banner, or in the vale
Robes in rich light the poplar pale.

Oft thy mavis, blithe and boon,

Cheers the morn and afternoon

With happy melodies, that seem

To turn to sound the sunny beam;

Or the nightingale apart

Flashes from his human heart,

Like earth-born lightning, ceaselessly,

Anguish, Hope, and Victory, .

In Southern isles where thro' balm shades

The moonlight glides o'er colonnades

Of marble, and the waters gush

In tuneful tears amid the hush

Of budding bowers, that silently

Slope thro' pale glory to the sea,

And in the calm and midnight dim

Seem listening to that threefold·hymn.

April, April, child of mirth

And sorrow, sweetest face on earth !

Oh ! had I such bright hopes to make

The wild woods listen for thy sake !

Oh ! had I spells to make thy pains

My glory, like thy sunlit rains,

My days a rainbow's arch, to climb

Far off from tears and clouds of Time !

# THE SKYLARK AND THE POET

How the blithe lark runs up the golden stair
  That leans thro' cloudy gates from heaven to
    earth,
And all alone in the empyreal air
  Fills it with jubilant sweet songs of mirth !
    How far he seems, how far
      With the light upon his wings !
    Is it a bird, or star
      That shines and sings ?

What matter if the days be dark and frore ?
  That sunbeam tells of other days to be;

And singing in the light that floods him o'er

  In joy he overtakes futurity :

      Under cloud arches vast

        He peeps, and sees behind

      Great summer coming fast

        Adown the wind.


And now he dives into a rainbow's rivers;

  In streams of gold and purple he is drown'd;

Shrilly the arrows of his song he shivers,

  As tho' the stormy drops were turned to

    sound :

      And now he issues thro',

        He scales a cloudy tower;

      Faintly, like falling dew,

        His fast notes shower.


Let every wind be hushed, that I may hear

  The wondrous things he tells the earth below;

Things that we dream of he is watching near,

    Hopes that we never dreamed he would

        bestow :

           Alas ! the storm hath rolled

             Back the gold gates again,

           Or surely he had told

             All heaven to men !

So the victorious poet sings alone,

    And fills with light his solitary home,

And thro' that glory sees new worlds foreshown,

    And hears high songs, and triumphs yet to

        come :

           He waves the air of Time

             With thrills of golden chords,

           And makes the world to climb,

             On linked words.

What, if his hair be grey, his eyes be dim,

    If wealth forsake him, and if friends be cold ?

Wonder unbars her thousand gates to him,

  Truth never fails, nor beauty waxeth old :

    More than he tells his eyes

      Behold, his spirit hears,

    Of grief, and joy, and sighs

      'Twixt joy and tears.


Blest is the man who with the sound of song

  Can charm away the heartache, and forget

The frost of penury and stings of wrong,

  And drown the fatal whisper of regret !

    Darker are the abodes

      Of kings, tho' his be poor,

    While Fancies, like the Gods,

      Pass thro' his door.


Singing, thou scalest heaven upon thy wings,

  Thou liftest a glad heart into the skies;

He maketh his own sunrise while he sings,

  And turns the dusty earth to Paradise :

I see thee sail along

   Far up the sunny streams;

Unseen, I hear his song,

   I see his dreams.

# THIRTY-FIRST OF MAY

AWAKE ! the crimson dawn is glowing;

   The blissful breath of morn

From golden seas is earthward flowing

   Thro' mountain peaks forlorn;

'Twixt the tall roses and the jasmine near,

   That darkly hover in the twilight air,

I see the glory streaming, and I hear

   The sweet wind whispering like a messenger.

'Tis time to sing ! the spirits of Spring

   Go softly by mine ear,

And out of Fairyland they bring

   Glad tidings to me here;

'Tis time to sing ! Now is the pride of youth
Pluming the woods, and the first rose appears,
And summer from the chambers of the south
Is coming up to wipe away all tears !

They bring glad tidings from afar
Of her that cometh after
To fill the earth, to light the air
With music and with laughter :
Ev'n now she leaneth forward, as she stands
And her fire-winged horses shod with gold
Stream, like a sunrise, from before her hands,
And thro' the Eastern gates her wheels are
rolled !

'Tis time to sing ! the woodlands ring
New carols day by day ;
The wild birds of the islands sing
Whence they have flown away :

'Tis time to sing—the nightingale is come;

   Amid the laurels chants he all night long,

And bids the leaves be still, the winds be dumb;

   How like the starlight flashes forth his song !


Immortal beauty from above,

   Like sunlight breathed on cloud,

Touches the weary soul with love,

   And hath unwound the shroud

Of buried Nature, till she looks again  .

   Fresh in infantine smiles and childish tears,

And o'er the rugged hearts of aged men

   Sheds the pure dew of youth's delicious years.


The heart of the awakened earth

   Breathes odorous ecstasy ;

Let ours beat time unto her mirth,

   And hymn her jubilee !

The glory of the universal soul

   Ascends from mountain tops and lowly flowers;

The mighty pulses throbbing thro' the whole

   Call unto us for answering life in ours.


Arise, young Queen of forests green !

   A path was strewn for thee

With hyacinth, and gold bells between,

   And red anemone :

Arise, young Queen of beauty and delight !

   Lift up in this fair land thy happy eyes;

For valleys yearn, and gardens for thy sight,

   But chief this heart that prays for thee with

     sighs.


   How oft into the opening blue

     I looked up wistfully,

   In hope to see thee wafted thro'

     Brights rifts of stormy sky :

         C

Many grey morns and nights and weary days,
  Without thy golden smile my heart was dying;
Oh ! in the valleys let me see thy face,
  And thy loose locks adown the woodwalks
    flying.


Come with thy flowers and silver showers,
  Thy rainbows and thy light;
Fold in thy robe the naked hours,
  And fill them with thy might :
Tho' less I seek thee for the loveliness
  Thou laughest from thee over land and sea,
Than for the hues wherein gay fancies dress
  My drooping spirit at the sight of thee.


  Come with thy voice of tears and joys,
    Thy leaves and fluttering wings !
  Come with the breezes, and the noise
    Of rivulets and of springs :

Tho' less I seek thee for thine harmonies

    Of winds and waters, and thy songs divine,

Than for that Angel that within me lies,

    And makes glad music echoing unto thine.

O gardens blossoming anew !

    O rivers and fresh rills !

O mountains in your mantles blue !

    O dales of daffodils !

What ye can do no mortal spirit can ;

    Ye have a strength within we cannot borrow :

Blessed are ye beyond the heart of man,

    Your joy, your love, your life beyond all

        sorrow !

# THE CLOUD

BRIGHT cloud, that springest from the laughing
  East,
   And on swift wings art come before the sun ;
   Thou infant that art panting to outrun
The God of Day; upon thy mother's breast
Wilt thou fall back, like an o'er-eager boy,
And die ere sunrise in the hope of joy ?

Or wilt thou climb the golden steep of day
   Into the zenith, like a conqueror, borne
   Upon the wheels of the ascending morn,
And gather power and glory by the way;
Yet, like a steed ere yet the goal be past,
Faint before noon with overmuch of haste ?

Or rather bask in the blue air of June,

    Till that fair-fashioned shape of thine, in

      seeming

    A king, a throned god, or angel dreaming,

Melt in the splendour of the summer noon,

Like drowsy warrior steept in sudden bliss

After sharp toil and fiery victories?


Or shall the afternoon beset thee round

    With thunders and with lightnings, till thy

      form

    Be mingled with the phantoms of the storm,

Thy lovely hues in black confusion drowned,

As some bright spirit from the height of fame

Hurled down in guilt, in sorrow, and in

    shame?


Or wilt thou wrap thy youth in every fold

    Of majesty till, veiling half the heaven,

Thou towerest o'er the world in purple and gold,

   King of the West from the peak of Even,

A blessed monarch, gracious and sublime,

Throned on the hearts of men and top of Time ?

# NOON

THE winds are hushed, the clouds have ceased
    to sail,
  And lie like islands in the ocean day;
  The flowers hang down their heads, and far
    away
A faint bell tinkles in the sun-drown'd vale :
No voice but the cicala's whirring note—
  No motion but the grasshoppers that leap—
The reaper pours into his burning throat
  The last drops of his flask, and falls asleep.

The rippling flood of a clear mountain stream
  Fleets by, and makes sweet babble with the
    stones;

The sleepy music with its murmuring tones
Lays me at noon in an Arcadian dream :
Hard by soft night of summer bowers is seen,
  With trellised vintage curtaining a cove,
Whose diamond mirror paints the amber-green,
  The glooming bunches, and the boughs above.


Finches and moths, and gold-dropt dragon-flies
  Dip in their wings, and a young village-
    daughter
Is bending with her pitcher o'er the water :
Her round arm imaged, and her laughing eyes,
And the fair brow amid the flowing hair,
  Look like the Nymph's for Hylas coming up,
Pictured among the leaves and fruitage there;
  Or the boy's self a-drowning with his cup.


Up through the vines, her urn upon her head,
  Her feet unsandal'd, and her dark locks free

She takes her way, a lovely thing to see;

And, like a skylark starting from its bed,

A glancing meteor, or a tongue of flame,

   Or virgin waters gushing from their springs,

Her hope flies up—her heart is free from blame—

   On wings of sound : she sings, oh ! how she

      sings !

# TO THE CICALA

BLITHEST spirit of the earth,
Happy as incarnate mirth,
Minion, whom the Fairies feed,
Who dost not toil and canst not need,
Thine odorous ark a forest bough;
While summer laughs as fair as now
I will not feast, or drink of wine,
But live with thee, and joys like thine.

Oh! who may be as blithe and gay
As thou, that singest night and day,
Setting the light and shadows green
A-flutter with thy pulses keen,

And every viney glen and vale

A-thrilling with thy long, long tale,

And river bank and starlit shore

With thy triumphs flooding o'er?

When the wild bee is at rest,

When the nightingale hath ceased,

Still I hear thee, reveller, still

Over heath and over hill:

Thou singest thro' the fire of noon,

Thou singest till the day be done,

Thou singest to the rising moon,

Thou singest up th' unrisen sun.

Into the forest I will flee,

And be alone with Mirth and thee,

And wash the dust from Fancy's wings

With tears of heaven, and virgin springs:

Thou shalt lead me o'er the tops

Of thymy hills, down orchard slopes,

Past sunlit dell, and moonlit river,
Thou shalt lead me on forever!

Lord of Summer, Forest-King!
Of the bright drops the breezes fling
Down upon the mossy lawn
In the dim sweet hours of dawn,
Clear as daylight, pure as heaven,
Drops which the mid-summer even
Weeps into pale cups silently,
I will take, and drink to thee!

Just as I raise it to my lip,
Plumed Oberon shall dip
His sceptre in, and Puck shall dive,
And I will swallow him alive;
And on the vapour of that dew
He shall rise, and wander thro'
My brain, and make a sudden light,
Like the first beam that scatters night.

Then shall I hear what songs they sing
Under the fresh leaves in the Spring;
And see what moonlit feasts they hold
Under a lily's roof of gold :
And when the midnight mists upcurl,
Watch how they whisk, and how they whirl,
And dance, and flash from earth to air
Bright and sudden as a star.

They shall dance and thou shalt sing :
But they shall slumber, court and king,
They shall faint ere thou be spent,
And each shall seek his dew-bell tent;
And Titania's self shall tire,
And sleep beneath a wild-rose briar,
Ere thou be sad, ere thou be still,
Piper of the thymy hill.

Oft at the first still flush of morn,
The soft notes of some charmed horn

I shall hear, like sounds in sleep,

Waft o'er the greenwood fresh and deep,

From magic hold, where giants thrall

Beauty in some airy hall,

And a plumed lover waits

To burst the spell before the gates.

When the sun is hot and high,

I will rest where low winds sigh,

And dark leaves twine, and rillets creep,

To send me, with thy whirr, asleep;

And softly on some prisoned beam,

Shall quiver down a noonday dream,

Wherein thy ceaseless note shall tingle,

And the sweet-toned waters mingle.

A dream of Faery, where a million

Of winged elves a rare pavilion

Build for Love amid the green,

The fairest summer-house e'er seen;

While some their silver trowels ring,
Others opal blocks shall bring,
And with quaint laugh and music fine,
Pile them in the sunny shine.

Monarch, thy great heart is more
Than treasuries, if thou be poor !
Tho' few the days that to thee fall,
They are long, and summer's all :
Minstrel, tho' thy life be brief,
Thou art happier than the chief
Of mortal poets, for thy song
Is fed with rapture all day long.

Thee, in thy fresh and leafy haunt,
Nor Wealth can bribe, nor Penury daunt,
Nor Glory puff, nor Envy tear,
Thy drink the dew, thy food the air :
Oh ! could I share in thy delight,
And dream in music day and night,

Methinks I would be even as thou,

And sing beneath a forest bough.

Nor pain nor evil canst thou see;

Thou fear'st not death, tho' it must be;

Therefore no sorrow lights on thee,

Or mingles with thy melody.

From want thy jocund heart is free,

Thou livest in triumphant glee,

Thou diest shouting jubilee !

A God—save immortality !

# TO A SUMMER FLY

Thou, that livest in the sun,
And, like the lilies, hast not spun,
Or toiled since thy life begun;
Thou that sorrow canst not see,
That fliest all shadows, swift and free
How can death o'ershadow thee?

If I were a fairy fine,
I would make a day of mine
Into a life as long as thine,
Fearless wanderer of the sky,
That art born, dost live and die,
Ere the bright days are gone by.

D

Through the livelong sunny day

Thou singest with thy lovers gay

To merry thoughts a merry lay;

Tiny thing, what tellest thou,

As thou glancest o'er me now,

Shedding down upon my brow


The diamond dust that sprinks thy wings?

Is it of the wondrous things

That the plumed summer brings

Out of her treasures? anthers fair,

Wherein the fallen shower-drops are

As blest elixirs rich and rare?


Tears of night, that in the beams

Of morning change to gold and gems?

Or odours like to wandering dreams,

That charm with subtlest spells, and take

Captive the heart, and then forsake,

Like songs we hear when half awake?

Oft thou bathest in clear well

Of the wild flower's brimming bell,

Cowslip, hyacinth, asphodel,

Silver rains, like nectar golden

In imperial vases holden

Of amber lilies, to embolden

Thy filmerings for their noonday flight

Up thro' the happy ether bright,

'Mid summer air and shoreless light;

I would feel the pangless pleasure

Thou feelest, when thou hast drunk a measure

Of the maydew at thy leisure;

Maydew by the morn served up

To thee in a violet cup,

Which, with loud murmurs thou dost sup,

Perfumed into ravishment

With the delicatest scent

From the inmost goblet lent.

There thou feastest in the shade

With linked rose and woodbine made,

Green glooms with chequering lights inlaid,

While the hours, like lovers, throng

Round dark-eyed Summer, lithe and strong,

And not a leaf shall fade for long.


I would feel the joy thou feelest,

As round the garden plots thou wheelest,

And, drunk with song and light, thou reelest,

And the noon is deep and fair,

And not a sound of life is there

But thy low chant that thrills the air.


Hast thou learnt those melodies

Heard when day comes up the skies,

And the subtle atomies

Are stirred with morning ?   Hath thy sight

Marked the shuttle of the night

Throw its threads across the light ?

At thy birth did that slim Fay,
That drew thy form at break of day
Out of the rose wherein it lay,
Swathe thee in the rainbow hues
Wherewith the level sunrise strews
That moment all the meadow dews?

Thou art a charmed bark that flees
Swiftly with songs thro' soundless seas,
With blossom odours for a breeze,
Launching from a green, green shore
The tiniest craft that ever bore
Silken sail, or silver oar.

Launching on a golden tide
Of morning, toward realms untried,
Thou pliest along the sunbeam wide,
Bound for some flowery cape afar,
Or sunflower-islet in mid air,
A dazzling dewdrop for thy star.

Oh wondrous life, oh winged spark !

Between thy plumes would I embark

What time the daybeam drives the dark :

If I were a fairy free

I would search the ethereal sea,

And sail far off with songs like thee.


If I were a fairy fine

I would make a day of mine

Into a life as long as thine,

Tearless wanderer of the sky,

That art born, dost live and die

Ere the summer days go by.

# THE FOREST

## I

In the hot hours, when scarce the whirr is heard
　Of the bird's wing, or murmur of the bee,
When the leaf shadows tremble on the sward,
　To the wild forest come away with me:
I know a dewy green where you may lie,
　　And dream you hear from the embowered
　　　glades
Low laughter twinkle, and sweet music sigh,
　And faint away among the pillar'd shades.

I know a lake upon whose surface pass ,
　Trembling soft pictures of the summer treen,

And as we gaze into that magic glass,

   The sloping woods with their high walks are

      seen;

Keep thou thine eye upon the azure water,

   And when its mirror ruffles with the air,

I'll show thee many a rosy forest-daughter,

   Satyr, and wild-eyed Hamadryad there.

I'll show thee sun-brown Faun with Wood-nymph

      playing,

   Or twining wreaths of eglantine and rose,

Or on soft moss the tawny musk grape laying

   For Pan, who takes his afternoon repose

Upon deep flowers and virgin green—to slake

   His thirsty ardours, when at set of day

From his enchanted dreams the God shall wake,

   And see the shadows turned the other way.

And sometimes Bacchus shall go reeling by

   Where the deep forest leaves a lawny dell,

With flute and twisted wand, and sunlit eye

   Amid the rose-crown'd Mænads, with a swell

Far off of mingled voices musical;

   And for a moment, in a stream of light,

Thou shalt behold the viney festival

   Sweep by like dream, and glitter out of sight.

If thou shouldst slumber in a thicket near,

   The grasshopper shall wake thee up with glee,

And hidden rillets bubbling in thine ear

   Shall float off the soft hours with melody:

Thy curls uplifted by the Zephyr sleek

   Shall make thee dream of some beloved hand

Laid on thy hair, a kiss upon thy cheek,

   And one dear face, the loveliest in the land.

## II

A sound of fluttering leaves begins to run

   From side to side, and the far-flying fawn

Glances athwart green glooms, or in the sun

　　Peers tremblingly, or shoots across a lawn:

From mossy glens, and tops of breezy hills

　　I hear the bugle wail, and bowstring keen;

Green plumes move with the leaves, wild

　　　　laughter thrills

From sylvan valleys and dark gulphs of green.


Look where the forest slopes unto the lake,

　　And the brisk winds that curl the summer

　　　　trees

Leap to the brink, their morning thirst to

　　　　slake,

　　Caught from the sharp rocks and the parched

　　　　leas:

The evening waters now begin to sing

　　Over the swart sands, and three Oreads tall

From oak-tree arms a crimson awning swing,

　　Whose ruby shadows o'er the mosses fall,

As tho' the blushing turf-plot saw, and knew

   The virgin huntress with unzoned limbs !

For now a lucent shoulder fresh with dew

   Dawns o'er the waters, as she shoreward
      swims:

Now leans she on the pebbles with her
   hand,

   And lifts herself amid her long bright hair;

Now with her nymphs she shoots across the
   strand,

   Peerless in grace and stature, pure and fair.


And now she sits in rosy light, and veils

   Her innocence, and to the silver sound

Of falling rillets she begins her tales

   Of Summer pastimes sought with horn and
      hound:

At every pause young girls with kirtles green,

   Taking their little lyres of gracious mould,

Sing  antique  songs,  and  strike  the  strings
   between—
Echoes, and shadows of the Age of Gold.

Oh ! I could tarry under these green boughs,
   In these deep coverts, all the summer long,
If only one sweet nymph with sunny brows
   Would teach me all her ancient woodland song;
Till I had learned such pure and simple breath,
   As, poured into the dusty ears of Kings,
Would make them thirsty for a wildrose wreath,
   Turf walks, and  thymy  slopes, and  fresh cold
     springs.

# THE FOUNTAIN

Fair fount, that singest in the air,
   And spinnest in the sun
Raiment for River Gods to wear,
   From dawn till day be done;
Oh! could I learn thy magic art, and share
Thy sympathetic sense, that moulds thee forms
So sweet in calm, so glorious in storms ;
Could beauty sway my speech, as thee the air !

Fair fount, thy music swift and strange,
   Thy lightnings in mine eyes,
Weave me with every sunny change
   Such pleasant phantasies,

That I, methinks, could dream away my years

Peacefully gazing, as thy silver dews

Make harmonies of lovely sounds and hues,

In answer to the soft wind as it veers.


Image of joy and flowing song,

   And fancy without measure,

Thy tongue is tuneful all day long,

   Thy heart leaps up with pleasure :

Thine is the glorious youth where jocund mind

Weaves tears with laughter, and regrets with

      hopes,

Whose careless moments, like thy sunny drops,

Are fancy-wooed, as they are by the wind.


But when the months have chained thy heart,

   And sealed thy tongue with frost,

An emblem of that day thou art

   When all we loved is lost :

'he heart of Age is but a frozen thing;

'he eyes of Age see but a wintry mist,

3y no sweet visions like thy sunbows kissed,

Whence smiles have fled, and tears have ceased

    to spring.

# THE POET AND FOUNT OF HAPPINESS

THERE is a fountain to whose flowery side
By divers ways the children of the earth
Come day and night athirst, to measure forth
Its living waters—Health and Wealth and Pride,
Power clad in arms and Wisdom argus-eyed :
But One apart from all is seen to stand,
And take up in the hollow of his hand
What to their golden vessels is denied,
Baffling their utmost reach.   He, born and nurst
In the glad sound and freshness of that place,
Drinks momently its dews, and feels no thirst ;
While, from his bowered grot or sunny space,
He sorrows for that troop, as it returns
Thro' the waste wilderness with empty urns.

# TO POESY

Tis not for golden eloquence I pray,
   A God-like tongue to move a stony heart :
   Full fain am I to dwell with thee apart
In solitary uplands far away,
And, thro' the blossoms of a bloomy spray,
   To gaze upon the wonderful, sweet face
   Of Nature in a wild and pathless place :
And if it were that I should once array,
In words of magic woven curiously,

   All the deep gladness of a summer morn,
Or rays of evening that light up the lea

   On dewy days of spring, or shadows borne
Athwart the forehead of an autumn noon—
Then would I die and ask no better boon !

                      E

# THE PROSPECT OF EVIL DAYS

'Tis not a time for triumph and delight,

For dance and song, for jocund thoughts and ease ;

Like cloud on cloud before a stormy night

Sorrows I see, and doleful deeds increase :

Destruction, like the Uragan, shall come,

And change, like mighty winds, whose lowering
      moan

Swells to a shout that makes the thunder dumb ;

And bloody Anarchs call the earth their own.

But when this time of terror and despair

Is past, tho' I be weary and o'erworn,

Still let me live to breathe the freshened air,

And hail the glory of that happy morn,

When the new day shall o'er the mountains roll,

And love again pour down his sunny soul !

# THE BLACKBIRD

How sweet the harmonies of afternoon !
   The blackbird sings along the sunny breeze
His ancient song of leaves, and summer boon;
   Rich breath of hayfields streams thro' whisper-
      ing trees;
And birds of morning trim their bustling wings,
And listen fondly while the blackbird sings.

How soft the love-light of the West reposes
   On this green valley's cheery solitude,
On the trim cottage with its screen of roses,
   On the grey belfry with its ivy hood,
And murmuring mill-race, and the wheel that
      flings
Its bubbling freshness—while the blackbird sings !

The very dial on the village church

    Seems as 'twere dreaming in a dozey rest;

The scribbled benches underneath the porch

    Bask in the kindly welcome of the West;

But the broad casements of the old Three Kings

Blaze like a furnace—while the blackbird sings.

And there beneath the immemorial elm

    Three rosy revellers round a table sit,

And thro' grey clouds give laws unto the realm,

    Curse good and great, but worship their own
        wit,

And roar of fights, and fairs, and junketings,

Corn, colts, and curs—the while the blackbird
    sings

Before her home, in her accustom'd seat,

    The tidy grandam spins beneath the shade

Of the old honeysuckle, at her feet

    The dreaming pug and purring tabby laid;

To her low chair a little maiden clings,
And spells in silence—while the blackbird sings.


Sometimes the shadow of a lazy cloud
   Breathes o'er the hamlet with its gardens
      green,
While the far fields, with sunlight overflow'd,
   Like golden shores of Fairyland are seen;
Again, the sunshine on the shadow springs,
And fires the thicket where the blackbird sings.


The woods, the lawn, the peaked manorhouse
   With its peach-covered walls, and rookery
      loud,
The trim, quaint garden alleys, screen'd with
      boughs,
   The lion-headed gates, so grim and proud,
The mossy fountain with its murmurings
Lie in warm sunshine—while the blackbird sings.

The ring of silver voices, and the sheen
  Of festal garments—and my Lady streams
With her gay court across the garden green;
  Some laugh, and dance, some whisper their
    love-dreams;
And one calls for a little page; he strings
Her lute beside her—while the blackbird sings.

A little while—and lo ! the charm is heard :
  A youth, whose life has been all Summer,
    steals
Forth from the noisy guests around the board,
  Creeps by her softly—at her footstool kneels;
And, when she pauses, murmurs tender things
Into her fond ear—while the blackbird sings.

The smoke-wreaths from the chimneys curl up
    higher,
  And dizzy things of eve begin to float

Upon the light; the breeze begins to tire;

  Half way to sunset with a drowsy note

The ancient clock from out the valley swings;

The grandam nods—and still the blackbird sings.


Far shouts and laughter from the farmstead peal,

  Where the great stack is piling in the sun;

Thro' narrow gates o'erladen waggons reel,

  And barking curs into the tumult run;

While the inconstant wind bears off, and brings

The merry tempest—and the blackbird sings.


On the high wold the last look of the sun

  Burns, like a beacon, over dale and stream;

The shouts have ceased, the laughter and the

    fun;

  The grandam sleeps, and peaceful be her

    dream !

Only a hammer on an anvil rings;

The day is dying; still the blackbird sings.

Now the good vicar passes from his gate

    Serene, with long white hair; and in his eye

Burns the clear spirit that hath conquer'd Fate,

    And felt the wings of immortality;

His heart is throng'd with great imaginings,

And tender mercies—while the blackbird sings.


Down by the brook he bends his steps, and

    thro'

    A lowly wicket; and at last he stands

Awful beside the bed of one, who grew

    From boyhood with him—who, with lifted

    hands,

And eyes, seems listening to far welcomings,

And sweeter music than the blackbird sings.


Two golden stars, like tokens from the Blest,

    Strike on his dim orbs from the setting sun;

His sinking hands seem pointing to the West;

He smiles as though he said ' Thy will be
  done ! '

His eyes, they see not those illuminings,

His ears, they hear not what the blackbird sings.

## THE POET TO A CAGED NIGHTINGALE

If I am sadder when I see thee sad
With rayless eyes, O summer-hearted bird,
Why do I weep when I behold thee glad
With inborn glory, and thy songs are heard ?
And, O young minstrel, I have seen thee stirred
With such immortal moments of delight,
That thine enchanted being hath appeared
To go forth on a carol, and take its flight
In answer to the call of some empyreal sprite !

When in a moment, as from dream awoke,
Thou didst begin to sing, and in such wise
As when the prime, inviolate forests broke
Forth into pæans, and with glad surprise

Struck unimaginable harmonies;

And the new-fashioned earth upsent a noise

Of tumult and of praise, and from the skies

Came down the manifold, melodious voice

Of Angels and of Gods, that sing, 'Rejoice,
     Rejoice!'

And then, descending from thy lofty tone,

Glorious as some sweet tempest, which in play

Apollo hath upraised around his throne,

Mocking the thunder and the winds, thy lay

Hath glided like a clear stream on its way,

A clear stream rushing on a golden floor,

And yet so swift that, when I bade thee stay

To run me once again that wild song o'er,

In swifter notes were drowned the notes that
     went before.

Then hadst thou beat thy prison-house in vain,

With idle wings, and prideful, angry eye,

Because thy gladness had become a pain,

And bound thee inly like an ecstasy ;

As tho' thou wert complaining—'Let me die,

For I am happy, happy, happy now ;

Oh ! let me wander forth upon the sky,

And fill the light with songs—oh ! let me go

Along the wide  sunbeam, and hear  the south

      winds blow ! '


At last, o'ermastered by thy strong desire

Of freedom, by vain hope, by sport and song,

Thou hast gazed round upon the golden wire

That girdled thee and broke thy spirit strong,

And sadness hath come over thee ere long,

And tears bedimmed the joyance of thine eyes,

As one who moaned—'oh ! wherefore is this wrong

Done to me ? think ye that my spirit dies ?

Ah ! but for these ill walls it would ascend the

      skies !

Know'st thou I come from summers of the South ?

Mine is a bluer air, a nobler sun ?

There are the friends and lovers of my youth,

Who shared my gladness till the day was done,

And soothed my brief unrests.   What hast thou
    done

To snatch me from society so dear ?

Where are   the   flowers   and   mountain-trees,
    whereon

I sate and sang for joy, and had no fear,

While songs as sweet as mine were thrilling in
    my ear ?


Do   not see far off the azure hills ?

Their aspect stirs me with a wild delight,

For there I know fresh fountains are, clear rills,

And by the waysides green young flowers and
    bright :

There the elated heart grows strong, despite

Of penury and care, for there the high
Eternal works of wonder are in sight,
Putting all lowly thoughts and passions by,
And wafting up the soul into the spanless sky.

Do I not hear the everlasting sea,
Whose murmur brings from the blue isles afar
Tidings of the flown summer unto me,
And hearts that throb beneath a happier star ?
Oh ! if strong love could sunder bolt and bar
Then would I live again one summer o'er,
And lave my wings in quenchless light and air,
My heart in blisses of my own sweet shore ;
Then flee where none should find, or cease for
        evermore ! '

But when I have approached thee in thy hour
Of darkness, and required with flattering tone
Melody in thy heaviness, the power
Of thy undying life to cheer my own,

A song when thou wert desolate and lone,

Dear minister of Pity, hast thou not

The sweetness of thy saddest thoughts foregone

To move me in my sorrow, and forgot

Captivity and tears, the burden of thy lot ?

If I could glad thee now by any spells

Of Phantasy, then would I fill thine ears

With all that the enraptured Poet tells

Of our strange hearts—the loves, the hopes, the
       fears,

The joys, the agonies of human years;

Or sing unto thee, but I never knew

Music so sweet as when it moves to tears :

Thy notes are brave as light that cleaves the
       blue,

And subtle as the air, and tender as the dew.

Ah ! me, I weep that thou, ordained for mirth,

To wander on wild wings, rejoice and soar,

And search with restless speed the heaven and
      earth,
To sing, to dream, to die and be no more,
Canst triumph like an angel, while I mourn
Who know that I shall never die, and more
Than Phantasy may vision, and can turn
From all I see and know, and feel myself forlorn.

For tho' sad sense of exile, and the sight
Of this thy prison sometimes makes thee pine,
Soon as thou hearst the winds, and seest the
      light,
Dost thou not kindle that lone heart of thine
With sunny song? oh! could I ravish mine
Or gladden others thus, I should not sigh
For evil dreams to torture me, like wine,
Into oblivious peace, to put away
The shadows of the past, or veil the coming
      day.

I weep that Man, with utterance more than thou,

A soul that searcheth farther than the wind,

A mind that, thro' the windows in his brow,

Can follow after the flown star, and find,

And from the shore of Time can see behind

Columns of fall'n Creations, and before

The great new Day whose coming splendours
     blind,

Should stoop for glistering serpents on that
     shore,

Nor see the coming tide, nor listen to its roar.


Sing me no songs, for I am sad at heart :

Thou art from God, and bountiful like Him :

But when I see thee mute, as now thou art,

It is as tho' thou saidst—' Mine eyes are dim

Thro' Man, whose heart is bitter to the brim,

Who hates the light, and poisons his own food,

Who was the next unto the Seraphim,

                      **F**

And now a bird can chide his thankless mood,

A little bird can say—" He envies me my good." '

Go forth, O winged Joy ! what ! shall I break

That liberal heart of thine, because my own

Lies quenched in dust and ashes ? I will wake

The God that sleeps within me, and put on

The long-disused arms that might have shone

Among sublimer spirits, and be free :

Go forth in light ! In love thou hast undone

Thine hopeless ill, and slain Adversity :

I thank thee for the shame thy songs have left

     in me.

# THE GLORY OF NATURE

IF only once the chariot of the Morn
    Had scattered from its wheels the twilight dun,
    But once the unimaginable Sun
Flashed godlike thro' perennial clouds forlorn,
And showed us Beauty for a moment born :

If only once blind eyes had seen the Spring
    Waking amid the triumphs of midnoon ;
    Or only once the lovely Summer boon
Pass by in state like a full-robed king,
The waters dance, the woodlands laugh and sing :

If only once deaf ears had heard the joy
    Of the wild birds, the morning breezes blowing,
    Or silver fountain from their caverns flowing,

Or the deep-voiced rivers rolling by ;
Then night eternal fallen from the sky :

If only once weird Time had rent asunder
   The curtain of the clouds, and shewn us Night
   Climbing into the awful Infinite
Those stairs whose steps are worlds, above and
      under,
Glory on glory, wonder upon wonder !

If Lightnings lit the Earthquake on his way
   But once, or Thunder spake unto the world ;
   The realm-wide banners of the Wind unfurled ;
Earth-prisoned fires broke loose into the day,
Or the great Seas awoke—then slept for aye !

Ah ! sure the heart of Man, too strongly tried
   By godlike Presences so vast and fair,
   Withering with dread, or sick with love's
      despair,

Had wept for ever, and to heaven cried,

Or struck with lightnings of delight had died !

But He, tho' heir of immortality,

   With mortal dust too feeble for the sight,

   Draws thro' a veil God's overwhelming light :

Use arms the soul—anon there moveth by

A more majestic Angel—and we die !

# THE MOUNTAINS

## I

Upon the icy mountain-top alone
   I only hear the beating of my heart;
Sunburst, and shower, and shadow, earthward
      thrown
Like mortal fortunes, for a moment shown,
   Go by me, and depart.

There is no voice to talk with me so high:
   The secret spirit of the desert place
Answers not to me; and beneath me lie
The world and all its wonders; Death and I
   Are standing face to face.

And from the torrents and the caves ascend

    Temple of cloud, dim king, and sunlit

    god,

Angels with aspects changing without end;

Visions of power and glory earthward bend,

    And sceptred giants nod.


A sunbeam cleaves the misty gulph, and lo !

    As thro' great gates unfolding in the sky,

Valleys, and plains, and rivers past me flow,

And silent cities, glittering from below,

    Like phantoms hover by.


So from the far-off mount of Poesy

    The world's great shows like the hushed

    champaign seem;

The Actual, unsubstantiality;

Real, what is shaped in Fancy's eager eye;

    Fear, love, a hope, a dream.

Glorious is he who on that sovranty

    Makes a far beacon of his soul sublime;

Blessed is he, who from th' illumined sky

Can reach the murmurs of Humanity,

    And hear the voice of Time.


## II

The spirit of the Poet, like the form

    Of the high mountains, cleaves the heavens

        asunder,

And flies into far realms of fear and wonder,

And howling wildernesses, where the storm

    Goes darkly with its thunder;


Or soars with quiet pinions where the light

    Of sun and stars, eternal and the same,

Awake afar the unapproached height,

Looks down serenely on the stormy night

    Of whirlwind, cloud, and flame.

Within the lone high places of his soul

    Love and Ambition, like the frost and sun,

    Pile up great towers, or drive the earth-

        quake on,

Let loose the winds, or bid the torrents roll,

    Or make the rivers run.


And when the proud world, tyrannous and

    strong,

    Tramples frail hearts into the dust of scorn,

    Rathe flowers of spring within his breast

    are born,

Fresh streams of pity murmur in his song,

    Fresh breezes of the morn.


The unborn future lightens on his brow,

    As on the topmost cliffs the dawning East;

    Memories, like glories poured back from the

    West,

Live in his heart, and in his music glow
    When summer days have ceased.

In his own land his ever-wakeful eye
    Stands sentinel, like an unsetting star;
The glory of his immortality,
Like the great peaks that glitter in the sky,
    Burns, and is shown afar.

And when vast cycles, rolling wars and woes,
    Have laid in darkness lesser lights between,
Far as the utmost age, or friends, or foes,
His mighty spectre, like th' eternal snows,
    Shall soar up and be seen.

# THE TEMPLE

A SHEPHERD-POET from a mountain land
  Near a proud temple's open portals stood;
By lavish steams of fragrance he was fanned ;
  He heard the hosannas of a mulitude.

The soaring temple seemed a holy world,
  And in its beauty was almost divine ;
He stood in wonder while the incense curled
  Round the tall columns and the golden shrine.

He heard the music rolling, like a flood
  On thunders based, with eddying echoes piled;
He saw the gaint shapes of man and God
  Glorious in domed sanctuaries isled.

He bowed his head, and all that glory shook
  His steadfast soul; but then he thought again
Of his green valley and its rippling brook,
  And the meek songs of poor and holy men.

Sweet words of peace and power, like blissful
      charms,
  The High Priest uttered from his carven throne,
And claspt his hands, and raised his purple arms,
  As tho' to teach humility by his own.

The shepherd bowed his head; that golden speech
  Sank, like a lovely melody, in his ears;
But then he thought how mountain hermits teach
  Love with rough words, but prove it with
      their tears.

He took his staff; he fled into the light,
  Far from that perilous beauty manifold,
Lest his enchanted ears and dazzled sight
  Should scorn the Presences they loved of old.

Beyond the city walls he fled in haste;

   He left its dust, its tumult, and its sound,

And soon beheld long vales and mountains vast,

   Their kingly heads with storm and lightning

     crown'd.

He saw the gulphy bosom of the woods

   Surge in the wind, and many a river wide

Glittering in silence, and the spanless floods

   Of ocean purpling on the other side.

He saw the plumed clouds go by in state,

   And shapes of mighty stature bodied forth,

Of pleading Angel, or of armed Fate,

   Throned in the air and gazing on the earth.

The soft wind stirred the grass and thickets green;

   Wild woodnotes stream'd around, rare odour-

     showers;

Glad springs and silver runnels lisped unseen

   Under the briary shades and tangled flowers.

He marked a shadow swallow up the day,
  Like coming judgment, and again the sun
Flash forth, and turn to gold the glooming grey,
  Like Mercy that repents ere ill be done.


And then he cried, ' Oh ! shall mine eyes forego
  The glorious temple of th' eternal skies
For all the frail magnificence below,
  The words of love for cobwebs of the wise ?


' Oh ! if their ears could hear, their eyes could see
  All that in this great world sublimes the heart,
Spirit, what need of other shrines for thee,
  Or muttered mysteries, or fantastic art ?


' When gilded shadows of the fancy win
  More lovers than the sacred face of Truth,
When o'er the ancient skeleton of Sin
  Lie the warm folds of beauty and of youth ;

' When juggling pomps and masked mockeries

    Ape the bold steps by freedom only trod,

When monstrous idols hide from human eyes

    The face of Nature and the throne of God ;


' Woe to that land, how bright soe'er it shine !

    Its air is thick with shapes that have no breath;

Tho' rich with milk and honey, corn and wine,

    Its name is Darkness and its King is Death.


' Better the icy wind, the sunshine dim,

    Better the thousand storms that shake the free,

The torrent thundering to the Sabbath hymn,

    Or the deep voice of the unchained sea !


' All-powerful Spirit, Universal King,

    Let others seek thee under marble piles,

Where the lamps tremble and the censers swing,

    And waved anthems stream thro' arched aisles.

'In that high Temple which Thyself didst frame
  And dost inhabit, I will look for Thee,
Whose roof is night, whose lamps are worlds of
    flame,
  Whose mighty bases are the earth and sea ;

'When Life and Death, thy ministers, attend,
  And with dread voices, chanting of all things,
From the great deep draw echoes without end,
  Immeasurable giants, clothed with wings.

'Thine orisons the world-wide voice that fills
  The morning air, the clouds thy censers be ;
Thine altars the inextinguishable hills ;
  Thy music is the thunder and the sea.

'On silent plains, on solemn shores untrod,
  Amid great mountains where it daily swells,
That holy music, I will worship God,
  And listen to His awful oracles.'

# THE GOLDEN CITY

## I

Two aged men, that had been foes for life,
  Met by a grave and wept—and in those tears
They washed away the memory of their strife;
  They wept again the loss of all the years.

Two youths, discoursing amid tears and laughter,
  Poured out their trustful hearts unto each
    other;
They never met before and never after,
  Yet each remembered he had found a brother.

A girl and boy amid the dawning light
  Glanced at each other at a palace door;

G

That look was hope by day, and dreams by night;
　And yet they never saw each other more.

Should gentle spirits born for one another
　Meet only in sad death, the end of all?
Should hearts that spring, like rivers, near each
　　other,
　As far apart into the ocean fall?

Should heavenly Beauty be a snare to stay
　Free love, and ere she hear his tongue com-
　　plain,
Forsake him, as a lily turns away
　From the air that cannot turn to it again?

Ah! hapless Zephyr, thou canst never part
　From the rare odour of the breathing bloom;
Ah! flower, thou canst not tell how fair thou
　　art,
　Or see thyself, or quaff thine own perfume.

Ah ! lover unbeloved, or loving not

    The doomed heart that only turns to thee;

In this wild world how cureless is thy lot !

    Who shall unwind the old perplexity ?


## II


Fond hearts, not unrequited shall ye be

    For ever I beheld a happy sight,

Heaven opened, and a starry company

    Far off, like Gods, and crowned sons of Light.


On beacon towers and citadels sublime

    They stood, and watched with their unsleeping

        eyes

Where two or three across the sea of Time

    Held on unto the shores of Paradise.


All day they rocked upon the stormy deep

    Till night beset them, and they could not tell

The signal lights—and they began to weep—
  Then the dark waters smote them, and they
    fell.

But oh! they woke in wonder! and behold
  A mighty city! 'twas a summer morn,
And dazzling sunshine smote on walls of gold,
  And blessed voices on their ears forlorn.

Soon as the grey prow touched upon the sands
  Wild birds from fadeless woods, and inland
    streams,
Showered o'er them those same notes of Faery
    lands
  Which they had heard in far, forgotten dreams.

And on the morning breezes come and part
  Gushes of those enchanted melodies,
Which, for brief moments, born within the heart,
  Made sad the earth with echoes of the skies.

Odours from silent fields of asphodel

    Breathe o'er them, steeping them in sudden
        bliss,

That once had touched their sense, as with a spell,

    And made them yearn for parted lives in this :


Visions which some pale bard had seen afar

    Burn in the sunset or the morning cloud,

And then depart into the scornful air,

    Leaving his heart with earthly sorrows bowed.


And men of sorrows, whose dejected eyes

    Had sought the earth and looked for death in
        vain,

Lifted their heads into the glorious skies,

    And sighed with perfect bliss unthralled of pain.


Then were they born into a vale of flowers,

    And heard infantine voices, and those tones

Linked in their hearts with the rejoicing hours

    Ere mortal anguish smit their weary bones.


Amid the tumult who are they that call

    In well - known tongues sweet welcomes?

        Who are they

Amid the multitudes that throng the wall

    With well-known faces, now so young and

    gay?


Who are the foremost on the shore to find,

    And clasp those weary mariners, pale with

    woes?

Friends, lovers, tender children, parents kind,

    Lost soon as loved—or loved too long to lose.


They took those storm-beat mariners by the

    hand,

    And thro' their worn and weary senses

    poured

Up to the golden Citadel they fare,

    And as they go their limbs are full of might,

And One awaits them on the topmost stair—

    One whom they had not seen, but knew at
        sight !

Hark ! there is music, such as never flowed

    Thro' all the Ages—for the Lost are found—

Sorrow is sitting by the throne of God,

    Justice and Mercy meet, and Love is
        crowned !

# TO THE POET

O GENTLE Poet, whosoe'er thou art,
  Whom God hath gifted with a loving eye
A sweet and mournful voice, a tender heart,
  Pass by the world, and let it pass thee by ;
Be thou to Nature faithful still, and she
Will be for ever faithful unto thee.

Let them disdain thee for thy just disdain ;
  Shield thou thy heart against the world accurst,
Where they discourse of joy, and ache with pain,
  And babble of good deeds, and do the worst ;
Shed dews of mercy on their wither'd scorn,
And touch their midnight darkness with thy
            morn.

There blind Ambition barters peace for praise ;

   There Pride ne'er sleeps, nor Hatred waxeth old;

And dwarfish Folly can his cubit raise

   To god-like stature on a little gold ;

There Madness is a king, and ev'n the wise

Sell truth to simpletons, and live on lies.


There pleasure is a sickly meteor-light,

   A star above, a pestilence below ;

There knowledge is a cup of aconite,

   That chills the heart and makes the pulses slow ;

Remorse, a scorpion's self-destroying sting,

Sorrow, a winter without hope of spring.


There Love's clear torch is quenched as in a

    tomb ;

   Or, bound for ever in a golden band,

He drags, with eyes fixt on his early doom,

   Behind lean Avarice, with the iron hand :

Fancy, that filled the woodlands with his glee,

Scorns at himself and murmurs to be free.


There Justice, mindless of her holy name,

   Creeps o'er the slime with adder's ears and eyes,

Stirs with dark hand the world-involving flame,

   Thirsteth for tears and hungers after sighs ;

There honour is a game to lose or win,

And sanctity a softer name for sin.


For thee 'tis better to remain apart,

   Like one who dwells beneath the forest green,

And heareth from afar the beating heart

   Of the wide world, all-seeing, though unseen,

In a cool cavern on a mountain side

With rare, sweet flowers and virgin springs

      supplied.


Hark thou the voices from the peopled plain

   In tuneful echoes murmuring in thine ears;

Watch thou the sunshine mingle with the rain,

   And mark how gladness interweaves with tears;

And ply thy secret, holy alchemy,

Like God, who gives the work, when none are by.

And from the twilight of thy solitude

   Note thou the lights and shadows of the sky,

And cast the mighty shapes of Evil and Good

   In perfect moulds of immortality,

Till they are seen from afar, like mountain light,

That burns on high when all below is night.

# DEATH AND THE SHEPHERD

Veil'd in a golden haze of afternoon
   The light is trembling o'er the western hills ;
   Hard by o'er rocks a mountain river spills
Its bubbling urn into the valley boon :
The pearly waters ruffle, as they run,
   In the soft spirit breathing from the south,
   And wild grapes, clustering o'er a cavern's
      mouth,
Flush with deep crimson in the evening sun.

The purple champaign, streaming like a sea,
   Far off between unfolding hills appears;
   The sound of a great city in our ears
Swells, like a sunken tide, melodiously :

And now and then the distant plain is stirred
  With bugle wail, or gleam of sylvan arms,
  Or grey smoke wreathing o'er the busy farms,
Or dusty breath of homeward-wending herd.


Under the forest roof the faint wind dies;
  The birds are still, the echoes are asleep;
  And thro' the arches green the sunbeams creep,
Floating the dizzy gnats and lazy flies :
An aged shepherd in an oaken shade
  Lay drowsily, and down the mossy ways
  He turned his dreaming eyes, and with amaze,
Fair shapes he saw, half glad and half afraid.


Shrill laughter from the grot is flooding forth
  Of two wild Oreads, whose large eyes shine
  Under clear temples shaded with the vine;
And good Silenus yields him to their mirth :
His arms are fettered in a jasmin band :

Forth from the curtains of each slumbrous lid

Shoot stars of joyance, often as they bid;

And the red cup is fallen from his hand.

He heard sweet sounds; he saw the graces dance:

'Ah! give me youth, and I will give to ye

All my peace-offerings to Adversity,'

He cried—and his white hair grew dark at once.

' 'Tis well,' he said, ' but what is flowing hair,

And strength, without the blisses fed by gold?

Plutus, for thee the firstlings of my fold

I will provide, so thou wilt hear my prayer.'

Then from amid the boughs the auspicious God,

Silently stretching forth his potent hand,

Flashed in the shepherd's eyes a golden wand,

As 'twere a sunbeam floating in the wood :

And therewithal was struck the caverned rock

Hid  in  wild  flowers  and  brambles  o'er  his

head;

And when he looked for dust there rained
    instead
Some fair round pieces down upon his flock.


Between the knotty boles brown Satyrs glanced,
    And star-eyed Fauns; and Momus, leaping
        out
    From the dark umbrage with an antic shout,
Made sport before the nymphs when they had
    danced :
Again he said, 'O gentle Momus, hear;
    I cannot laugh with them, nor yet be merry;
    For I have thoughts within I cannot bury;
Grant that, and thou shalt have three goats
    a year.'


From the dry leaves he started up in haste;
    He danced and laughed, and laughed and
    danced; but still

Relentless memory ! when the heart is evil

Nought is so cheerless as a merry devil;

My heavy thoughts are fetters to my feet.'


A cold wind sighed among the trees, and Death

Lifted his crowned head o'er a branch of pine

Screening his armed hand in leaves of vine :

Softly, 'Why prayedst thou not to me?' he saith

'Oh ! whatsoever thou art !' the old man cried

'I have done deeds that haunt me, in my
youth;

Yield me, pale Power, oblivïon of the truth,

That I may live !' Death touched him, and he
died.

# FOLLOW NOW

## I

ONE morning of the breezy spring,
   With jocund hearts and free,
We met old Time a-wandering
   By the shores of the Great Sea ;
The waters dashed before the wind,
   Onwards he still did fare :
He seemed a beggar old and blind,
   With neither joy nor care.

We knew not our Arch-enemy,
   For we were heedless boys ;
So we called to join our revelry
   The Lord of tears and sighs ;

H

'Father,' our wanton voices sung,
  'With us thou shalt abide ;
Upon the shoulders of the young
  Full swiftly shalt thou ride.'

He sped not for our merriment,
  He sped not for our laughter ;
With frolic steps we forward went;
  Old Time he laboured after ;
At last a voice like broken thunder
  Came rolling on the wind ;
Still we stood 'twixt fear and wonder—
  He spake—his words were kind.

'Children, my pace is old and slow,
  My blood is thin and cold ;
Have pity on me—haste not so—
  Have mercy on the old ;
My songs and tales ye cannot hear
  If ye leave me here behind '—

But we laughed and fled when he came near,

And his voice went down the wind.

' Know ye not I have magic charms

Hid in my wallet here ?

Wizard spells to save from harms,

And spoils of every year ?

Rare essences, green leaves of truth,

Elixirs, gems, and gold ?

Odours and balmy drops for youth,

And balsams for the old ? '

The image of the rising sun

Fled o'er the glittering sands,

And running seemed to bid us run,

And catch him in our hands ;

It seemed the very fire of joy,

Wherewith our hearts ran o'er,

Made visible unto the eye,

And dancing on before.

'Come, father, come and make us game,'
  We shouted, nought afraid;
And, thinking he was blind and lame,
  Snares in his path we laid ;
Onward he stept, and took no harm
  From any ills we planned,
But he seized us with his mighty arm
  And flung us on the sand.

A wild rose chain, in frolic freak,
  With linked woodbines tied,
We wove, and cast it o'er his neck,
  The blind old man to guide;
We pulled him on with all our might;
  The flower links snapt in twain;
The roses scattered left and right,
  But we joined the links again.

All day the giant made us merry ;
  And at the set of day

Still joyous all were we, nor weary
  For all our sunny play :
Lightly we coursed, and from the brow
  Of a primrose-covered hill
We shouted, 'Father, follow now !'
  But his steps were slower still.


## II

Again we met, but it was noon—
  And now the unruffled sea
Basked in the full midsummer sun,
  And proud as noon were we ;
The dewy ripples to the sand
  In pleasant murmurs rolled ;
One came, and took us by the hand,
  A traveller blithe and bold.

He said, 'When last ye walked with me,
  In the springtime long ago,

As swift as antelopes were ye,

    While I was faint and slow ;

I have thrown by my crutched staff,

    And ye have gat ye strength,

So I can run and leap and laugh,

    And race with ye at length.

We cried, 'Art thou that blind old man

    We met beside this sea,

Who couldst not follow when we ran,

    Or make us walk with thee ?

Oh ! thou art changed !'   'Not I,' he said,

    'Who am for ever strong ;

Ye thought me old in infancy,

    In youth ye think me young.'

He seemed as one 'twixt youth and age;

    Cheeks dark with toil, but bright;

His eyes, his brow, a mystic page,

    His limbs of knotty might :

His locks were rich as autumn trees,

    But touched with frosts of ill;

Lips smiling with accustomed ease,

    Or locked with iron will.

'My life is not as yours,' he said,

    'My growth is not the same—

Ye see my wrinkled hoary head,

    Ye hear my hollow name;

Ye think that I am ever old,

    An idle, useless hack;

But thus it is—when ye go on,

    My children, I go back!'

And then he bade us race with him,

    As we had bade him once,

When our young limbs were light and slim

    And his but weary bones :

But he kept pace with us, and ran

    Along that well-known shore;

'O friend,' we cried, 'O mighty man,

    We cannot mock thee more !

'Forgive us; we outran thee then—

    But tell us, whence hast thou

Gat thee this strength and speed, and when

    Those dark locks on thy brow?'

'When ye were babes ye thought me old :

    Farewell again,' he said;

'I shall return; farewell!' behold

    He waved his hand and fled !

### III

And now the summer afternoon

    Flamed in the golden west;

The dying airs were soft and boon,

    Like sighings for their rest;

Our feet were slow upon the shore

    Where we so oft had run;

And now the day had little more

   Before the setting sun.

And one came bounding from the hills,

   A bugle in his hand;

Shouting he leapt the little rills,

   And stood upon the strand.

He blew his horn, he called his hounds,

   Less wearied he than they;

His dark curls hid his forehead round,

   But ours were fleckt with grey.

' Hail, friends, young friends of mine, I ween !

   What have ye done this day ?

Among the mountains I have been,

   And marked the eaglets play;

And yet I bid you to a race

   Again on these smooth shores

And ye shall weary of my pace

   As once I did of yours ! '

'Boast not!' we said, for we were tried
  To anger by his taunt;
'Thou hast not beaten yet,' we cried;
  'Let who shall vanquish vaunt :'
And stretching on with struggling might}
  We gained a step or two;
But he came up as swift as light,
  And shouted 'Follow now!'


## IV


The sun was sunk, the day was done :
  Th' horizon far away
In mighty rivers seemed to run
  Heart's blood of dying day :
A star or two shone over all—
  The full moon, like a wraith,
Rose ghastly on the mountain wall ;
  I felt its icy breath.

saw my image shadowed there
  Upon the moonlit sands,
ſy sunken brows, my snowy hair,
  My lean and trembling hands :
ınd then I thought upon that morn,
  Midday, and afternoon,
ːre those dear friends were from me borne
  Whom I shall follow soon.

sighed, and near me stood a child,
  Like me, on that fair day
Vhen we with merriment beguiled
  The pilgrim old and grey :
looked—oh ! was it magic art
  That showed me that young elf?
'he form alike in every part
  To that was once myself?

'he roses on the lip, the gold
  Upon the flowing hair,

The supple limbs of gracious mould?
  All, all were living there :
The silver tongue, the truthful face,
  The artless, early words
Stirred me, like echoes in the bass
  Of a harp's treble chords.

And with a quaint smile he began :
  ' Old man, wilt run with me,
As once ye bade that ancient man
  Ye met beside the sea ? '
' And who art thou ? ' I asked in fear,
  ' Who seest thro' my heart ?
Thou wert not born when he was here;
  Oh ! tell me who thou art ? '

And still his words they were the same—
  ' Old man, wilt run with me ?
Come, father, come and make me game,
  As once he did to thee !

'My child,' I said, 'my pace is slow,
  My blood is thin and cold;
Have pity on me, haste not so—
  Have mercy on the old!'

He laughed a moment; then he stood
  As one prepared for flight;
His aspect took an awful mood,
  His frame a giant's might:
He spread forth wings, I saw his eyes,
  Like starlight throb and glow—
And, as he rose into the skies,
  He thundered 'Follow now!'

# WOMEN AND CHILDREN

God said, 'Bring little children unto me' ;
   And Man is likest God, when from his heart
Truth flows in its divine simplicity,
   And love dwells in him, working without art :
Children are earth's fair flowers—the crown of
      life
   A noble woman, and he is refilled
With hope who turns with love unto his wife,
   With love who turns with hope unto his child.

If never faces were beheld on earth
   But toiling manhood, and repining age,
No welcome eyes of innocence and mirth
   To look upon us kindly, who would wage

The gloomy battle for himself alone?

   Or thro' the dark of the o'erhanging cloud

Look wistfully for light? Who would not groan

   Beneath his daily task, and weep aloud?

But little children take us by the hand,

   And gaze with trustful cheer into our eyes;

Patience and Fortitude beside us stand

   In woman's shape, and waft to heaven our

      sighs :

The guiltless child holds back the arm of Guilt

   Upraised to strike, and woman may atone

With sinless tears for sins of man, and melt

   The damning seal when evil deeds are done.

When thirsty suffering hath drunk up our tears,

   And left the heart sere as an autumn leaf,

From her fond eyes they fall for us; she cheers

   With songs, and lights with hope, the cloud of

      grief :

When our sweet Youth for ever buried li

  And we wellnigh forget the thing we v

Once more we meet him in the young blt

  And laugh to see his resurrection there

When to the ear of Vengeance or of Hati

  We yoke ill thoughts, and memories h

    Hell,

'Tis she that stays us, like relenting Fate

  'Tis her weak arm that locks the

    wheel :

Above the dust of conflict, and the jar,

  She lifts a little child ; her voice is heai

Piercing above the thunders of the war,

  'Spare thou, that thine hereafter m

    spared ! '

And should they go before us on that way

  Which all must tread, and leave us fain

    sorrow;

Should the great light of Love forsake the day,

   Memory's bright moon bespeaks a sunlight

      morrow :

Behold, the skies unfold ! broad beams descend;

   Beneath the Gods upon the golden stair,

Amid the upward glories without end,

   At heaven's gate they stand, and bid us there.

# THE COMING DAY

On Sinai's steep I saw the morning cloud,
    Shattered with light, roll off on either hand,
    And on the topmost peak an Angel stand,
That lifted up his arms, and cried aloud,
    And shook the sea and land.

The Night is ended, and the Morning nears:
    Awake, look up! I hear the gathering sound
    Of coming cycles, like an ocean round;
I see the glory of a thousand years
    Lightening from bound to bound.

Woe, woe! the earth is faint; its heart is old,
    And none look upward. Where is one who
    saith,

'Forgive my sins by reason of my faith?'
Where is one truthful bard, one prophet bold,
    One heart that listeneth?

One holy soul that prayeth night and morn,
    One kindly hermit, or one lowly sage,
    One adamantine warrior, who can wage
A steadfast war, without the arms of scorn,
    Against a scornful Age?

Where is the promise of the world's great youth,
    The sunrise of the soul, when God's own eye
    Scattered the darkness of futurity,
And kings bowed down, and caught the light of
    truth
    Directly from on High?

The hour is come again; the world-wide voice
    Of God shall cry unto the ears of time:
    Scorners shall seek, and saints shall welcome
    Him,

And know the ancient Presence, and rejoice,
    As in the days of prime.


And they that dwell apart shall know each
    other ;
    And they that hymn their solemn songs
    alone
    Shall hear far voices mingling with their
    own,
And understand the utterance of a brother
    In every tongue and tone.


And countless tongues upon a note of
    praise
    Shall hang, until, like thunder in the
    hills
    Redoubled and redoubled, it fulfils
The earth, and heaven, and everlasting days,
    And drowns the noise of ills.

That note shall soar from every living heart;

That endless note shall never die away:

God, only God, to-day as yesterday!

Thou wert from everlasting, and thou art

For ever and for aye!

# THE HARVEST HOME

Come, let us mount the breezy down,
And hearken to the tumult blown
Up from the lowland and the town.

Lovely lights, smooth shadows sweet
Swiftly o'er croft and valley fleet,
And flood the hamlet at our feet,—

Its grove, its hall, its grange that stood
When Bess was Queen, its steeple rude,
Its mill that patters in the wood ;

And follow where the brooklet curls
Seaward, or in cool shadow whirls,
Or silvery o'er its cresses purls.

The harvest days are come again,

The vales are surging with the grain,

The merry work goes on amain.


Pale streaks of cloud scarce veil the blue,

Against the golden harvest hue

The Autumn trees look fresh and new.


Wrinkled brows relax with glee,

And aged eyes they laugh to see

The sickles follow o'er the lea.


I see the little kerchief'd maid

With  dimpling cheek, and boddice staid,

'Mid the stout striplings, half afraid :


Her red lip, and her soft blue eye

Mate the poppy's crimson dye,

And the cornflower waving by.

I see the sire with bronzed chest ;
Mad babes amid the blithe unrest
Seem leaping from the mother's breast.

The mighty youth, and supple child
Go forth ; the yellow sheaves are piled,
The toil is mirth, the mirth is wild !

Old head, and sunny forehead peers
O'er the warm sea, or disappears,
Drown'd amid the waving ears ;

Barefoot urchins run, and hide
In hollows 'twixt the corn, or glide
Towards the tall sheaf's sunny side ;

Lusty Pleasures, hobnail'd Fun
Throng into the noonday sun,
And 'mid the merry reapers run.

Draw the clear October out,
Another, and another bout,
Then back to labour with a shout !

The banded sheaves stand orderly
Against the purple autumn sky,
Like armies of Prosperity.

Hark ! through the middle of the town,
From the sunny slopes run down
Bawling boys and reapers brown :

Laughter flees from door to door,
To see fat Plenty with his store
Led a captive by the poor,

Fetter'd in a golden chain,
Rolling in a burly wain,
Over valley, mount, and plain :

Right through the middle of the town,
With a great sheaf for a crown,
Onward he reels, a happy clown.

Faintly cheers the tailor thin,
And the smith with sooty chin
Lends his hammer to the din;

And the master, blithe and boon,
Pours forth his boys that afternoon,
And locks his desk an hour too soon.

Yet, when the shadows eastward seen,
O'er the smooth-shorn fallows lean,
And Silence sits where they have been,

Amid the gleaners I will stay,
While the shout and roundelay
Faint off, and daylight dies away;

Summers parted, glories flown;

Till day beneath the West is roll'd,
Till grey spire, and tufted wold
Purple in the evening gold.

Memories, when old age is come,
Are stray ears that fleck the gloom,
And echoes of the Harvest-home.

# THE ELEVENTH OF SEPTEMBER

SISTER, the Daystar, that hath brought me hither,
   Once more thy birthday, shines on me and thee,
   And by its welcome light I seem to see
The many years that we have sped together,
Winter and summer, still the selfsame weather.

Tho' mountains sunder, and the wild sea flings
   Its desert 'twixt our hearts—and on the wind
   Thy voice is still, so musical and kind;
Tho' world-wide tumults drown, and Time's grey
     wings
Shadow the past, thy spirit to me sings!

Thou art mine own self with a softer frame,
   A clearer brow, and eyes more full of thought;

Thou art myself into an angel wrought,
Thy heart an altar, whence the purest flame,
Of hope ascends, for ever and the same.

Thou art my dearest and my first of kin :
    The thoughts of man are riddles, but my heart
    Tells me in all most truly what thou art :
Thou hast a secret loadstar deep within,
Whereto I thrill in spite of care and sin.

When cruel passion tore me I could see
    Thy pleading eyes, and hear thy tuneful tongue;
    When crafty counsels flattered me to wrong,
Justice and Truth with voices clear and low
Spoke to me from the temple of thy brow.

To thy pure, simple songs I loved to lend
    My ear; at thy soft pity's healing word
    My spirit sheathed at once its angry sword;
And to thy blessed meekness I could bend
A heart which many tyrants could not rend.

The wise world looked, and, seeing dark and
      bright,
  Deemed that in spirit we remained apart :
  But we were but as adverse stars, that dart
Their beams into each other, and unite
Aspects of different omen in one light.

Thy beauty is the shrine where Mercy dwells ;
  Thy tongue Love's tender oracle below,
  Whence his immortal inspirations flow;
Thine eyes the lightnings, whose soft glory quells
Pride that disdains, and Anger that rebels.

As the sun-colour and the crystalline
  Mingle together in the summer green—
  Nature that shall be and hath ever been,
My heart's quick motions, and the peace of thine
Make one pure love eternal and divine !

# FLIGHT OF THE SWALLOW

THE golden-throated merle and mellow thrush
    Chant to us yet ; the woodlark will not fly
His ancient sylvan solitude, or hush
    His dewy pipings for a softer sky :
      But the swallow flies away ;
      I would that I were he ;
      He follows the flown May
        Across the sea.

The swallow hath a fickle heart at best ;
    He bears off the sweet days he brought us o'er,
And sounds retreat like an ungrateful guest,
    That shuns the flattered host he sued before :

Should kind Mirth be forgot

When his dark locks are grey,

And Love remembered not ?

Ah ! stay, oh ! stay.'

Know ye of gladness, that with jocund hearts

Can cast away old loves for love of new ?

O friends, the music of a thousand art

Charms not so sweetly as a voice that's true :

I sang ye songs of sorrow ;

I sang ye songs of glee;

I cried, ' Await to-morrow ' ;

Ye heard not me.

Know ye of sorrow ?   Can ye understand

Mortality, that hung unto the robe

Of Summer, as she flies from land to land,

Follow swift Youth around the rolling globe ?

Joy's winged heart is light,

But blind are his bright eyes;

Grief seeth in the night
Of tears and sighs.


The feathers of Time's wings, ere yet they fall
Ye pluck, and from his plumes ye trim your
own;
Ye answer to the south wind's silver call;
Ah! whither wend ye, leaving me alone?
Ah! stay, dear friends, ah, stay,
And leave me not forsaken;
Care takes not the same way
That ye have taken.


In our lorn woods the morn and evensong
Will fail, and things of sunshine cease to be:
Lo! chilling Winter leadeth Death along;
I see the tyrant shake his lance at me.
Delight hath fled the earth,
The evil days are come,

K

So I will light my hearth,

   And sing at home.

Ye seek the blue isles, and the happy hills;

   Ye rush into the heart of summer skies;

Ye leave behind ye unremember'd ills;

   Ye fly, like happy souls, to Paradise.

     Oh ! could ye, blissful things,

       On my dark, utter day,

     Lend me those selfsame wings

       To flee away !

# EVENING

Hush ! it is Even, dark-eyed Even,
  With her low song, and tender sigh,
Soft-uttered voice of earth to heaven,
  Witnessed by one lone star on high;
On wheels of rayless flame she passeth by;
  And Peace sits by her, clasped unto her heart;
  Hatred, relent; and, Care, forget thy smart;
    And, Anger, droop thine eye.

Dusky Memories throng her way;
  Bright Fancies from the shadows peep;
And Hopes that panted in the day
  Sadly hide their eyes and weep :

Lorn Griefs look up into the balmy sky;

Plumed Love upon the soundless air comes
out;

And Wit he bears his wavering lamp about;

Despair seeks where to die.

Fly with her yon howling cave

Loud with riot, red with flame,

Where haggard Passions whirl and rave,

And Phrenzy links her arms with shame :

Revenge uncoils the serpents round him curled,

Red Murder steals abroad with perilous hand;

And Treason whispers grim, and lights his
brand

To fire a slumbering world.

Fly with her the golden doors,

Thro' whose valves thrown open wide

The trumpet-streaming revel pours

Where Folly haunts the ears of Pride :

And Nature, like the king at Babylon,

Dazzled with glories, with enchantments bound,

Hears not the momently-increasing sound

Of Judgment rolling on.

Rather let us rove with her

By river-slopes and orchards green,

Where soft and fragrant thickets stir,

And the last daylights gush between :

Or, when the tides are sunken to their bed,

Wave her godspeed upon the silent sands,

As she sails on, far off to other lands,

And Night is Queen instead.

Rather, while all the air is mute,

And flowers breathe rare from closing bells,

Let us listen to her lute,

And hear her sing divine farewells ;

While failing echoes fall upon our ears,

Forever dying thro' the misty hills,

And mix with murmurs of the mountain rills,
   And Twilight drops her tears.

Rather with her seek the chamber
   Which fond Hesper, twinkling thro'
The vines that o'er the lattice clamber,
   Every moment peeps into :
Where some kind mother softly steals above,
   From friend, and lover, to her sleeping boy,
   And on his cheek, all flushed with dreams of joy,
     She sets her seal of love.

Sometimes let us seek the cell
   Where the Poet, far apart,
To two or three he loveth well
   Works the wonders of his art :
And from his coloured lamp and golden lyre
   Peoples the past with voices and with light,
   And scrolls futurity's unfathomed night
     With symbols and with fire.

And when the stars are o'er us burning,

 And the moon is dawning slow,

And the nightingale is mourning,

 From his porch we'll softly go :

And memories of his music shall descend

 With the pure spirits of the sunless hours,

 Sink thro' our hearts, like dew into the flowers

 And haunt us without end.


Blessed art thou, O dark-eyed Even,

 Thou and thy tender handmaids true;

Send us thy mercies down from heaven

 Daily with the falling dew :

Dark flowers to heal the bleeding brows of

 sorrow

 From thy soft chaplets fail not to untwine,

 And pour into our tortured hearts, like wine,

 Sweet dreams until to-morrow.

# THE GARLANDS OF MEMORY

WHEN Memory in the gloom of cyprus bowers
    Unwove her garlands, she laid down with sighs
Mournfully, one by one, the withered flowers
    That were at morn the light of her sad eyes :
The wild buds she had gathered had drunk up
    Their matin dew, and died ; grey dust of death
Lay desolate in the lily's silver cup ;
    The red rose breathed not its voluptuous
        breath :
    She said, ' The light is dying,
      'Tis nigh the end of day ;
    Cease, heart, oh ! cease thy sighing,
      We must away, away ! '

Their drooping graces and their dusky hues,

   Their faint sweets telling of the morning time,

Pleaded to her so well she could not choose

   But love them faded better than their prime ;

She held them up before her aching sight,

   She breathed fond sighs to spread them out

      again ;

She laid their dim, soft leaves across the light,

   And gave them tender tears like autumn rain:

     She sang, ' The sun is leaving

      The blessed summer day ;

      Cease, heart, ah ! cease thy grieving,

      We must away, away ! '


Then blamed she the swift sun, whose eager touch

   Had stolen all their beauty's early treasure;

The wind that had been wanton overmuch,

   And drawn their life forth with excess of

     pleasure :

Her tears could not awake their bloom again;

   In vain against her mournful heart they lay;

Her tenderest tears could wash away no stain ;

   Her beating heart but shed their leaves away :

      She moaned, 'The sun is setting,

         It is the end of day ;

      Cease, heart, ah ! cease regretting,

         We must away, away ! '


At last she found some leaves of eglatere,

   Whose circling spray had bound those flowers

      in one :

She said, 'I will not weep while thou art here,

   Whose odour and fresh leaf outlives the sun;

Green wert thou in the early morning shine;

   Green art thou still at even—a holy wreath

Of pale, sweet flowers for me thou still may'st

      twine,

   When I go forth to be the bride of Death ! '

She sighed, ' The sun is set,

It is no longer day;

Oh ! heart, couldst thou forget !

But come, away, away ! '

# THE HOLYTIDE

THE days are sad ; it is the Holytide :

    The flowers have ceased to blow, and birds
        to sing :

Where shall the weary heart of man abide

    Save in the jocund memories of the spring ?

As the grey twilight creeps across the snow

    Let us discourse of walks when leaves were
        green :

Methinks the roses are more sweet, that blow

    In Memory's shade, than any that are seen.


The days are sad : it is the Holytide :

    Drear clouds have hid the crimson of the
        West,

And, like the winged day, delight hath died
  Within me, and proud passions gone to rest :
In this dark hour, before the lamps are lit,
  Thro' the heart's long, long, gallery I will go,
And mark pale Memory's taper full on it,
  Starting strange hues, like firelight on the
    snow.

The days are sad : it is the Holytide :
  Ye, whom I may not see for evermore,
Oh ! I will dream, tho' Death's great waste is
    wide,
  That ye may hear me from your silent shore :
And ye who wander, and are far apart,
  (Oh ! this great world is bleak, and years are
    growing,)
I have a sunny corner in my heart
  Where I do set ye when rough winds are
    blowing.

The days are sad : it is the Holytide :
 There is a welcome in the porch—I hear
The voice of one whom I have loved and tried,
 A voice I have not heard this many a year :
Ah ! me, that face is like the withered flowers,
 Paler with pain, with sorrows more forlorn ;
But still the smile, the soul of other hours,
 Shines from that face, the even like the morn.

The days are sad : it is the Holytide :
 We speak together while the daylight dies :
I see not he is old, for to my side
  The ghost of Youth comes up between our
   sighs :
The charm is broken by a single word—
  He answers—'Thou wilt hear no more on
   earth
The faithful voice that we so oft have heard,
 Or see that face that was the sun of mirth !'

The days are sad : it is the Holytide :

   Now let the last words of departed friends

Be sweeter to thee than a singing bride ;

   Weigh hearts, and for oblivion make amends :

Spurn not the penitent with haggard eye ;

   Seat thou the hungry outcast by thy chair ;

The  son  whose  spring  hath  fled  in  tempest

      by,

   The weeping daughter with dishevelled hair.


The days are sad : it is the Holytide :

   Let Wealth and Glory, as they take their fill,

Mark how Mischance to Fortune is allied;

   Let Hope look up again thro' cloud of ill :

Let us look down into our children's eyes,

   And think, amid the mirth and festal flow,

How  once  we  were  as  they  are—think  with

      sighs

   Of them that were as we are, long ago.

The days are sad : it is the Holytide :

   Cleanse off the ills of Time, the hates of years ;

Hush forked Scorn, and veil the crest of Pride;

   Kiss humble Love, and wipe away his tears;

Let vain things be forgot for evermore;

   Let good things rise from out these mournful

      days;

Bring out forsaken memories from thy store,

   If there be any pity, any praise.


The days are sad : it is the Holytide :

   Ah ! let the Grief, that knocks against thy gate,

Sit by thy heart, and murmur at thy side,

   Think of Truth, think of Mercy, think of Fate;

Think what kind dews have fallen on thy head;

   What thou wouldst do, but what thou hast

      not done;

Cast out the flaunting Sirens, that have led

   Thy heart, and once for all, and every one.

The days are sad : it is the Holytide :

    Hark ! in the drifting tempest, and the roar

Of darkling waters, are the Powers that guide

    The wreck of Nature to a summer shore;

Let Man too in the darkness arm, and strive

    With the dark host within him, rise and fight,

And, ere the morrow morn, begin to live;

    Sorrow brings strength, as day is born of
        night.


The days are sad ; it is the Holytide :

    The sun is on the hearth, the world at
        home ;

Over the frozen heath the whirlwinds ride ;

    Drink to the past, and better days to come :

Wreathe we our goblets with the evergreen,

    Fadeless as truth, sad as humanity ;

Let no bright flower or withered leaf be seen ;

    These hours are sisters to Adversity.

                     L

The days are sad : it is the Holytide :

    The winter morn is short, the night is long ;

So let the lifeless hours be glorified

    With deathless thoughts, and echoed in sweet

        song :

And thro' the sunset of this purple cup

    They will resume the roses of their prime,

And the old dead will hear us, and wake up,

    Pass with dim smiles, and make our hearts

        sublime !


The days are sad : it is the Holytide :

    Be dusky mistletoes and hollies strown,

Sharp as the spear that pierced His sacred

        side,

    Red as the drops upon his thorny crown ;

No haggard passion, and no lawless mirth

    Fright off the sombre Muse—tell sweet old

        tales,

Sing songs, as we sit bending o'er the hearth,

Till the lamp flickers, and the memory fails.


The days are sad : it is the Holytide :

But ere we part to dreams this blessed night,

Of Angel songs on the hushed mountain side,

And wondrous shapes that come upon the
light,

Let us lift up our voices altogether

In one deep harmony, a rapt farewell,

So sweet we shall not hear the stormy weather,

And dying sorrow wake to hear it swell.


THE END

# ERRATA

Page 49, 2nd stanza for 'Fearless' read 'Tearless.'
,, 51, ,, for 'filmerings' read 'film-wings.'
,, 62, ,, for 'where jocund' read ' 'whose jocund.'
,, 77, 1st line bottom stanza, insert 'I' between 'Do' and 'not,'
,, 99, line 6, insert a colon after 'for ever :'
,, 138, 4th stanza, insert a comma after 'shadows,'
,, 140, line 1, delete comma at end of line
,, 162, 3rd line from bottom 'his' should be 'His.'

**JOHN LANE**

THE
BODLEY
HEAD
VIGO Sᵀ
W.
Telegrams
"BODLEIAN
LONDON"

E.H.NEW.

CATALOGUE of PUBLICATIONS
in BELLES LETTRES all at net prices

# List of Books

IN

## *BELLES LETTRES*

(*Including some Transfers*)

# Published by John Lane

### 𝔗𝔥𝔢 𝔅𝔬𝔡𝔩𝔢𝔶 𝔥𝔢𝔞𝔡

VIGO STREET, LONDON, W.

*N.B.—The Authors and Publisher reserve the right of reprinting any book in this list if a new edition is called for, except in cases where a stipulation has been made to the contrary, and of printing a separate edition of any of the books for America irrespective of the numbers to which the English editions are limited. The numbers mentioned do not include copies sent to the public libraries, nor those sent for review.*

*Most of the books are published simultaneously in England and America, and in many instances the names of the American Publishers are appended.*

————◆————

ADAMS (FRANCIS).

    ESSAYS IN MODERNITY. Crown 8vo. 5s. net. [*Shortly.*
        Chicago: Stone & Kimball.
    A CHILD OF THE AGE. (*See* KEYNOTES SERIES.)

ALLEN (GRANT).

    THE LOWER SLOPES: A Volume of Verse. With Title-page and Cover Design by J. ILLINGWORTH KAY. 600 copies. Crown 8vo. 5s. net.
        Chicago: Stone & Kimball.
    THE WOMAN WHO DID. (*See* KEYNOTES SERIES.)
    THE BRITISH BARBARIANS. (*See* KEYNOTES SERIES.)

BAILEY (JOHN C).

    AN ANTHOLOGY OF ENGLISH ELEGIES. [*In preparation.*

**BEARDSLEY (AUBREY).**

THE STORY OF VENUS AND TANNHÄUSER, in which is set forth an exact account of the Manner of State held by Madam Venus, Goddess and Meretrix, under the famous Hörselberg, and containing the adventures of Tannhäuser in that place, his repentance, his journeying to Rome, and return to the loving mountain. By AUBREY BEARDSLEY. With 20 full-page Illustrations, numerous ornaments, and a cover from the same hand. Sq. 16mo. 10s. 6d. net. [*In preparation.*

**BEDDOES (T. L.).**

*See* GOSSE (EDMUND).

**BEECHING (REV. H. C.).**

IN A GARDEN: Poems. With Title-page designed by ROGER FRY. Crown 8vo. 5s. net.
New York: Macmillan & Co.

**BENSON (ARTHUR CHRISTOPHER).**

LYRICS. Fcap. 8vo, buckram. 5s. net.
New York: Macmillan & Co.

**BRIDGES (ROBERT).**

SUPPRESSED CHAPTERS AND OTHER BOOKISHNESS. Crown 8vo. 3s. 6d. net.
New York: Charles Scribner's Sons.

**BROTHERTON (MARY).**

ROSEMARY FOR REMEMBRANCE. With Title-page and Cover Design by WALTER WEST. Fcap. 8vo. 3s. 6d. net.

**BUCHAN (JOHN).**

MUSA PISCATRIX. [*In preparation.*

**CAMPBELL (GERALD).**

THE JONESES AND THE ASTERISKS. (*See* MAYFAIR SET.)

**CASE (ROBERT).**

AN ANTHOLOGY OF ENGLISH EPITHALAMIES.
[*In preparation.*

**CASTLE (MRS EGERTON).**

MY LITTLE LADY ANNE. (*See* PIERROT'S LIBRARY.)

**CASTLE (EGERTON).**

*See* STEVENSON (ROBERT LOUIS).

**CRAIG (R. MANIFOLD).**

THE SACRIFICE OF FOOLS: A Novel. Crown 8vo. 4s. 6d. net. [*In preparation.*

CRANE (WALTER).

> Toy Books. Re-issue. Each with new Cover Design and
> end papers. 9d. net.
>> The group of three bound in one volume, with a decora-
>> tive cloth cover, end papers, and a newly written and
>> designed preface. 3s. 6d. net.
>> I. This Little Pig.
>> II. The Fairy Ship.
>> III. King Luckieboy's Party.
>>> Chicago : Stone & Kimball.

CROSSE (VICTORIA).

> The Woman who Didn't. (*See* Keynotes Series.)

DALMON (C. W.).

> Song Favours. With a Title-page designed by J. P.
> Donne. Sq. 16mo. 3s. 6d. net.
>> Chicago : Way & Williams.

D'ARCY (ELLA).

> Monochromes. (*See* Keynotes Series.)

DAVIDSON (JOHN).

> Plays : An Unhistorical Pastoral ; A Romantic Farce ;
> Bruce, a Chronicle Play ; Smith, a Tragic Farce ;
> Scaramouch in Naxos, a Pantomime, with a Frontis-
> piece and Cover Design by Aubrey Beardsley.
> Printed at the Ballantyne Press. 500 copies. Small
> 4to. 7s. 6d. net.
>> Chicago : Stone & Kimball.

> Fleet Street Eclogues. Fcap. 8vo, buckram. 5s.
> net.                          [*Out of Print at present.*

> A Random Itinerary and a Ballad. With a Fron-
> tispiece and Title-page by Laurence Housman.
> 600 copies. Fcap. 8vo, Irish Linen. 5s. net.
>> Boston : Copeland & Day.

> Ballads and Songs. With a Title-page and Cover
> Design by Walter West. Third Edition. Fcap.
> 8vo, buckram. 5s. net.
>> Boston : Copeland & Day.

DAWE (W. CARLTON).

> Yellow and White. (*See* Keynotes Series.)

DE TABLEY (LORD).
  POEMS, DRAMATIC AND LYRICAL. By JOHN LEICESTER
    WARREN (Lord De Tabley). Illustrations and Cover
    Design by C. S. RICKETTS. Second Edition. Crown
    8vo. 7s. 6d. net.
      New York: Macmillan & Co.
  POEMS, DRAMATIC AND LYRICAL. Second Series, uni-
    form in binding with the former volume. Crown 8vo.
    5s. net.
      New York: Macmillan & Co.
DIX (GERTRUDE).
  THE GIRL FROM THE FARM. (*See* KEYNOTES SERIES.)
DOSTOIEVSKY (F.).
  *See* KEYNOTES SERIES, Vol. III.
ECHEGARAY (JOSÉ).
  *See* LYNCH (HANNAH).
EGERTON (GEORGE).
  KEYNOTES. (*See* KEYNOTES SERIES.)
  DISCORDS. (*See* KEYNOTES SERIES.)
  YOUNG OFEG'S DITTIES. A translation from the Swedish
    of OLA HANSSON. With Title-page and Cover Design
    by AUBREY BEARDSLEY. Crown 8vo. 3s. 6d. net.
      Boston: Roberts Bros.
FARR (FLORENCE).
  THE DANCING FAUN. (*See* KEYNOTES SERIES.)
FLEMING (GEORGE).
  FOR PLAIN WOMEN ONLY. (*See* MAYFAIR SET.)
FLETCHER (J. S.).
  THE WONDERFUL WAPENTAKE. By 'A SON OF THE
    SOIL.' With 18 full-page Illustrations by J. A.
    SYMINGTON. Crown 8vo. 5s. 6d. net.
      Chicago: A. C. M<sup>c</sup>Clurg & Co.
FREDERIC (HAROLD).
  MRS ALBERT GRUNDY. (*See* MAYFAIR SET.)
GALE (NORMAN).
  ORCHARD SONGS. With Title-page and Cover Design
    by J. ILLINGWORTH KAY. Fcap 8vo, Irish Linen.
    5s. net.
    Also a Special Edition limited in number on hand-made paper
    bound in English vellum. £1, 1s. net.
      New York: G. P. Putnam's Sons.

GARNETT (RICHARD).

POEMS. With Title-page by J. ILLINGWORTH KAY. 350 copies. Crown 8vo. 5s. net.
   Boston : Copeland & Day.

DANTE, PETRARCH, CAMOENS, cxxiv Sonnets rendered in English. Crown 8vo. 5s. net. [*In preparation.*

GEARY (NEVILL).

A LAWYER'S WIFE: A Novel. Crown 8vo. 4s. 6d. net. [*In preparation.*

GOSSE (EDMUND).

THE LETTERS OF THOMAS LOVELL BEDDOES. Now first edited. Pott 8vo. 5s. net.
Also 25 copies large paper. 12s. 6d. net.
   New York : Macmillan & Co.

GRAHAME (KENNETH).

PAGAN PAPERS : A Volume of Essays. With Title-page by AUBREY BEARDSLEY. Fcap. 8vo. 5s. net.
   Chicago : Stone & Kimball.

THE GOLDEN AGE. Crown 8vo. 3s. 6d. net.
   Chicago : Stone & Kimball.

GREENE (G. A.).

ITALIAN LYRISTS OF TO-DAY. Translations in the original metres from about thirty-five living Italian poets, with bibliographical and biographical notes. Crown 8vo. 5s. net.
   New York : Macmillan & Co.

GREENWOOD (FREDERICK).

IMAGINATION IN DREAMS. Crown 8vo. 5s. net.
   New York : Macmillan & Co.

HAKE (T. GORDON).

A SELECTION FROM HIS POEMS. Edited by Mrs MEYNELL. With a Portrait after D. G. ROSSETTI, and a Cover Design by GLEESON WHITE. Crown 8vo. 5s. net.
   Chicago : Stone and Kimball.

HANSSON (LAURA MARHOLM).

MODERN WOMEN : Six Psychological Sketches. [Sophia Kovalevsky, George Egerton, Eleanora Duse, Amalie Skram, Marie Bashkirtseff, A. Edgren Leffler.] Translated from the German by HERMIONE RAMSDEN. Crown 8vo. 3s. 6d. net. [*In preparation.*

HANSSON (OLA). *See* EGERTON.

HARLAND (HENRY).
GREY ROSES. (*See* KEYNOTES SERIES.)

HAYES (ALFRED).
THE VALE OF ARDEN AND OTHER POEMS. With a
Title-page and a Cover designed by E. H. NEW.
Fcap. 8vo. 3s. 6d. net.
Also 25 copies large paper. 15s. net.

HEINEMANN (WILLIAM).
THE FIRST STEP. A Dramatic Moment. Small 4to.
3s. 6d. net.

HOPPER (NORA).
BALLADS IN PROSE. With a Title-page and Cover by
WALTER WEST. Sq. 16mo. 5s. net.
Boston : Roberts Bros.
A VOLUME OF POEMS. With Title-page designed by
PATTEN WILSON. Sq. 16mo. 5s. net.
[*In preparation.*

HOUSMAN (CLEMENCE).
THE WERE WOLF. With six Full-page Illustrations,
Title-page and Cover Design, by LAURENCE HOUS-
MAN. Sq. 16mo. 4s. net. [*In preparation.*

HOUSMAN (LAURENCE).
GREEN ARRAS : Poems. With Illustrations by the
Author. Crown 8vo. 5s. net. [*In preparation.*

IRVING (LAURENCE).
GODEFROI AND YOLANDE : A Play. With three Illus-
trations by AUBREY BEARDSLEY. Sm. 4to. 5s. net.
[*In preparation.*

JAMES (W. P.).
ROMANTIC PROFESSIONS : A Volume of Essays. With
Title - page designed by J. ILLINGWORTH KAY.
Crown 8vo. 5s. net.
New York : Macmillan & Co.

JOHNSON (LIONEL).
THE ART OF THOMAS HARDY : Six Essays. With Etched
Portrait by WM. STRANG, and Bibliography by JOHN
LANE. Second Edition. Crown 8vo. 5s. 6d. net.
Also 150 copies, large paper, with proofs of the portrait. £1, 1s.
net.
New York : Dodd, Mead & Co.

JOHNSON (PAULINE).

WHITE WAMPUM : Poems.   With a Title-page and Cover
Design by E. H. NEW.   Crown 8vo.   5s. net.
Boston : Lamson, Wolffe & Co.

JOHNSTONE (C. E.).

BALLADS OF BOY AND BEAK.   With a Title-page designed
by F. H. TOWNSEND.   Sq. 32mo.   2s. 6d. net.
[*In preparation.*

KEYNOTES SERIES.

Each volume with specially designed Title-page by AUBREY
BEARDSLEY.   Crown 8vo, cloth.   3s. 6d. net.

Vol.   I. KEYNOTES.   By GEORGE EGERTON.
[*Seventh edition now ready.*
Vol.   II. THE DANCING FAUN.   By FLORENCE FARR.
Vol.   III. POOR FOLK.   Translated from the Russian of
F. Dostoievsky by LENA MILMAN.   With a Preface
by GEORGE MOORE.
Vol.   IV. A CHILD OF THE AGE.   By FRANCIS ADAMS.
Vol.   V. THE GREAT GOD PAN AND THE INMOST
LIGHT.   By ARTHUR MACHEN.
[*Second edition now ready.*
Vol.   VI. DISCORDS.   By GEORGE EGERTON.
[*Fourth edition now ready.*
Vol.   VII. PRINCE ZALESKI.   By M. P. SHIEL.
Vol.   VIII. THE WOMAN WHO DID.   By GRANT ALLEN.
[*Eighteenth edition now ready.*
Vol.   IX. WOMEN'S TRAGEDIES.   By H. D. LOWRY.
Vol.   X. GREY ROSES.   By HENRY HARLAND.
Vol.   XI. AT THE FIRST CORNER AND OTHER STORIES.
By H. B. MARRIOTT WATSON.
Vol.   XII. MONOCHROMES.   By ELLA D'ARCV.
Vol.   XIII. AT THE RELTON ARMS.   By EVELYN SHARP.
Vol.   XIV. THE GIRL FROM THE FARM.   By GERTRUDE
DIX.
Vol.   XV. THE MIRROR OF MUSIC.   By STANLEY V.
MAKOWER.
Vol. XVI. YELLOW AND WHITE.   By W. CARLTON
DAWE.
Vol. XVII. THE   MOUNTAIN   LOVERS.   By   FIONA
MACLEOD.
Vol. XVIII. THE WOMAN WHO DIDN'T.   By VICTORIA
CROSSE.               [*Second edition now ready.*

KEYNOTES SERIES—*continued.*
*The following are in rapid preparation.*
Vol. XIX. THE THREE IMPOSTORS. By ARTHUR
MACHEN.
Vol. XX. NOBODY'S FAULT. By NETTA SYRETT.
Vol. XXI. THE BRITISH BARBARIANS. By GRANT ALLEN.
Vol. XXII. IN HOMESPUN. By E. NESBIT.
Vol. XXIII. PLATONIC AFFECTIONS. By JOHN SMITH.
Vol. XXIV. NETS FOR THE WIND. By UNA TAYLOR.
Vol. XXV. ORANGE AND GREEN. By CALDWELL LIP-
SETT.
Boston : Roberts Bros.

KING (MAUDE EGERTON).
ROUND ABOUT A BRIGHTON COACH OFFICE. With 30
Illustrations by LUCY KEMP WELCH. Cr. 8vo.
5s. net. [*In preparation.*

LANDER (HARRY).
WEIGHED IN THE BALANCE : A Novel. Crown 8vo.
4s. 6d. net. [*In preparation.*

LANG (ANDREW). *See* STODDART.

LEATHER (R. K.).
VERSES. 250 copies. Fcap. 8vo. 3s. net.
*Transferred by the Author to the present Publisher.*

LE GALLIENNE (RICHARD).
PROSE FANCIES. With Portrait of the Author by
WILSON STEER. Fourth Edition. Crown 8vo.
Purple cloth. 5s. net.
Also a limited large paper edition. 12s. 6d. net.
New York : G. P. Putnam's Sons.
THE BOOK BILLS OF NARCISSUS, An Account rendered
by RICHARD LE GALLIENNE. Third Edition. With
a Frontispiece. Crown 8vo. Purple cloth. 3s. 6d. net.
Also 50 copies on large paper. 8vo. 10s. 6d. net.
New York : G. P. Putman's Sons.
ROBERT LOUIS STEVENSON, AN ELEGY, AND OTHER
POEMS, MAINLY PERSONAL. With Etched Title-page
by D. Y. CAMERON. Cr. 8vo. Purple cloth. 4s. 6d. net.
Also 75 copies on large paper. 8vo. 12s. 6d. net.
Boston : Copeland & Day.
ENGLISH POEMS. Fourth Edition, revised. Crown 8vo.
Purple cloth. 4s. 6d. net.
Boston : Copeland & Day.

**LE GALLIENNE (RICHARD).**

RETROSPECTIVE REVIEWS, A LITERARY LOG, 1891-1895.
2 vols. crown 8vo. Purple cloth. 9s. net.
*[In preparation.*
New York : Dodd, Mead & Co.

GEORGE MEREDITH : Some Characteristics. With a Bibliography (much enlarged) by JOHN LANE, Portrait, etc.
Fourth Edition. Cr. 8vo. Purple cloth. 5s. 6d. net.

THE RELIGION OF A LITERARY MAN. 5th thousand.
Crown 8vo. Purple cloth. 3s. 6d. net.
Also a special rubricated edition on hand-made paper. 8vo.
10s. 6d. net.
New York : G. P. Putnam's Sons.

**LIPSETT (CALDWELL).**

ORANGE AND GREEN. (*See* KEYNOTES SERIES.)

**LOWRY (H. D.).**

WOMEN'S TRAGEDIES. (*See* KEYNOTES SERIES.)

**LUCAS (WINIFRED).**

A VOLUME OF POEMS. Fcap. 8vo. 4s. 6d. net.
*[In preparation.*

**LYNCH (HANNAH).**

THE GREAT GALEOTO AND FOLLY OR SAINTLINESS. Two Plays, from the Spanish of JOSÉ ECHEGARAY, with an Introduction. Small 4to. 5s. 6d. net.
Boston : Lamson, Wolffe & Co.

**MACHEN (ARTHUR).**

THE GREAT GOD PAN. (*See* KEYNOTES SERIES.)
THE THREE IMPOSTORS. (*See* KEYNOTES SERIES.)

**MACLEOD (FIONA).**

THE MOUNTAIN LOVERS. (*See* KEYNOTES SERIES.)

**MAKOWER (STANLEY V.).**

THE MIRROR OF MUSIC. (*See* KEYNOTES SERIES.)

**MARZIALS (THEO.).**

THE GALLERY OF PIGEONS AND OTHER POEMS. Post 8vo. 4s. 6d. net. *[Very few remain.*
*Transferred by the Author to the present Publisher.*

**MATHEW (FRANK).**

THE WOOD OF THE BRAMBLES : A Novel. Crown 8vo.
4s. 6d. net. *[In preparation.*

## THE MAYFAIR SET.

Each volume fcap. 8vo. 3s. 6d. net.

Vol. I. THE AUTOBIOGRAPHY OF A BOY: Passages selected by his Friend, G. S. STREET. With a Title-page designed by C. W. FURSE.

*[Fourth Edition now ready.*

Vol. II. THE JONESES AND THE ASTERISKS: a Story in Monologue. By GERALD CAMPBELL. With Title-page and six Illustrations by F. H. TOWNSEND.

Vol. III. SELECT CONVERSATIONS WITH AN UNCLE NOW EXTINCT. By H. G. WELLS. With Title-page by F. H. TOWNSEND.

*The following are in preparation.*

Vol. IV. THE FEASTS OF AUTOLYCUS: The Diary of a Greedy Woman. Edited by ELIZABETH ROBINS PENNELL.

Vol. V. MRS ALBERT GRUNDY: Observations in Philistia. By HAROLD FREDERIC.

Vol. VI. FOR PLAIN WOMEN ONLY. By GEORGE FLEMING.

New York : The Merriam Company.

## MEREDITH (GEORGE).

THE FIRST PUBLISHED PORTRAIT OF THIS AUTHOR, engraved on the wood by W. BISCOMBE GARDNER, after the painting by G. F. WATTS. Proof copies on Japanese vellum, signed by painter and engraver. £1, 1s. net.

## MEYNELL (MRS.), (ALICE C. THOMPSON).

POEMS. Fcap. 8vo. 3s. 6d. net. *[Out of Print at present.*
A few of the 50 large paper copies (First Edition) remain, 12s. 6d. net.
THE RHYTHM OF LIFE AND OTHER ESSAYS. Second Edition. Fcap. 8vo. 3s. 6d. net.
A few of the 50 large paper copies (First Edition) remain, 12s. 6d. net.
*See also* HAKE.

## MILLER (JOAQUIN).

THE BUILDING OF THE CITY BEAUTIFUL. Fcap. 8vo. With a Decorated Cover. 5s. net.

Chicago : Stone & Kimball.

## MILMAN (LENA).

DOSTOIEVSKY'S POOR FOLK. (*See* KEYNOTES SERIES.)

MONKHOUSE (ALLAN).
  BOOKS AND PLAYS : A Volume of Essays on Meredith,
    Borrow, Ibsen, and others. 400 copies. Crown 8vo.
    5s. net.
        Philadelphia : J. B. Lippincott Co.

MOORE (GEORGE).
  See KEYNOTES SERIES, Vol. III.

NESBIT (E.).
  A POMANDER OF VERSE. With a Title-page and Cover
    designed by LAURENCE HOUSMAN. Crown 8vo.
    5s. net.
        Chicago : A. C. McClurg & Co.
  IN HOMESPUN. (See KEYNOTES SERIES.)

NETTLESHIP (J. T.).
  ROBERT BROWNING : Essays and Thoughts. Third
    Edition. With a Portrait. Crown 8vo. 5s. 6d. net.
    New York : Chas. Scribner's Sons.

NOBLE (JAS. ASHCROFT).
  THE SONNET IN ENGLAND AND OTHER ESSAYS. Title-
    page and Cover Design by AUSTIN YOUNG. 600
    copies. Crown 8vo. 5s. net.
    Also 50 copies large paper. 12s. 6d. net.

O'SHAUGHNESSY (ARTHUR).
  HIS LIFE AND HIS WORK. With Selections from his
    Poems. By LOUISE CHANDLER MOULTON. Por-
    trait and Cover Design. Fcap. 8vo. 5s. net.
        Chicago : Stone & Kimball.

OXFORD CHARACTERS.
  A series of lithographed portraits by WILL ROTHENSTEIN,
    with text by F. YORK POWELL and others. To be
    issued monthly in term. Each number will contain
    two portraits. Parts I. to VI. ready. 200 sets only,
    folio, wrapper, 5s. net per part ; 25 special large
    paper sets containing proof impressions of the por-
    traits signed by the artist, 10s. 6d. net per part.

PENNELL (ELIZABETH ROBINS).
  THE FEASTS OF AUTOLYCUS. (See MAYFAIR SET.)

PETERS (WM. THEODORE).
  POSIES OUT OF RINGS. Sq. 16mo. 3s. 6d. net.
                                [In preparation.

PIERROT'S LIBRARY.
> Each volume with Title-page, Cover Design, and End-papers designed by AUBREY BEARDSLEY. Sq. 16mo. 2s. 6d. net.
> *The following are in preparation.*
> Vol. I. PIERROT. By H. DE VERE STACPOOLE.
> Vol. II. MY LITTLE LADY ANNE. By Mrs EGERTON CASTLE.
> Vol. III. DEATH, THE KNIGHT AND THE LADY. By H. DE VERE STACPOOLE.
> Vol. IV. SIMPLICITY. By A. T. G. PRICE.
> Philadelphia : Henry Altemus.

PISSARRO (LUCIEN).
> THE QUEEN OF THE FISHES. A Story of the Valois, adapted by MARGARET RUST, being a printed manuscript, decorated with pictures and other ornaments, cut on the wood by LUCIEN PISSARO, and printed by him in divers colours and in gold at his press in Epping. Edition limited to 70 copies, each numbered and signed. Crown 8vo, on Japanese handmade paper, bound in vellum, £1 net.

PLARR (VICTOR).
> IN THE DORIAN MOOD : Poems. Crown 8vo. 5s. net.
> *[In preparation.*

PRICE (A. T. G.).
> SIMPLICITY. (*See* PIERROT'S LIBRARY.)

RADFORD (DOLLIE).
> SONGS AND OTHER VERSES. With Title-page designed by PATTEN WILSON. Fcap. 8vo. 4s. 6d. net.
> Philadelphia : J. B. Lippincott Co.

RAMSDEN (HERMIONE).
> *See* HANSSON.

RICKETTS (C. S.) AND C. H. SHANNON.
> HERO AND LEANDER. By CHRISTOPHER MARLOWE and GEORGE CHAPMAN. With Borders, Initials, and Illustrations designed and engraved on the wood by C. S. RICKETTS and C. H. SHANNON. Bound in English vellum and gold. 200 copies only. 35s. net.
> Boston : Copeland & Day.

RHYS (ERNEST).
> A LONDON ROSE AND OTHER RHYMES. With Title-page designed by SELWYN IMAGE. 350 copies. Crown 8vo. 5s. net.
> New York : Dodd, Mead & Co.

ROBERTSON (JOHN M.).
> ESSAYS TOWARDS A CRITICAL METHOD. (New Series.)
> > Crown 8vo. 5s. net. [*In preparation.*

ROBINSON (C. NEWTON).
> THE VIOL OF LOVE. With Ornaments and Cover Design
> > by LAURENCE HOUSMAN. Crown 8vo. 5s. net.
> > Boston : Lamson, Wolffe & Co.

ST. CYRES (LORD).
> THE LITTLE FLOWERS OF ST. FRANCIS: A new ren-
> > dering into English of the Fioretti di San Francesco.
> > Crown 8vo. 5s. net. [*In preparation.*

SHARP (EVELYN).
> AT THE RELTON ARMS. (*See* KEYNOTES SERIES.)

SHIEL (M. P.).
> PRINCE ZALESKI. (*See* KEYNOTES SERIES.)

SMITH (JOHN).
> PLATONIC AFFECTIONS. (*See* KEYNOTES SERIES.)

STACPOOLE (H. DE VERE).
> PIERROT. (*See* PIERROT'S LIBRARY.)
> DEATH, THE KNIGHT AND THE LADY. (*See* PIERROT'S
> > LIBRARY).

STEVENSON (ROBERT LOUIS).
> PRINCE OTTO. A rendering in French by EGERTON
> > CASTLE. Crown 8vo. 5s. net. [*In preparation.*
> > Also 100 copies on large paper, uniform in size with the Edinburgh
> > Edition of the Works.
> A CHILD'S GARDEN OF VERSES. With nearly 100
> > Illustrations by CHARLES ROBINSON. Crown 8vo.
> > 5s. net. [*In preparation.*

STODDART (THOS. TOD).
> THE DEATH WAKE. With an Introduction by ANDREW
> > LANG. Fcap. 8vo. 5s. net.
> > Chicago : Way & Williams.

STREET (G. S.).
> THE AUTOBIOGRAPHY OF A BOY. (*See* MAYFAIR SET.)
> MINIATURES AND MOODS. Fcap. 8vo. 3s. net.
> > *Transferred by the Author to the present Publisher.*
> > New York : The Merriam Co.

SWETTENHAM (F. A.).
> MALAY SKETCHES. With Title-page and Cover Design
> > by PATTEN WILSON. Crown 8vo. 5s. net.
> > New York : Macmillan & Co.

SYRETT (NETTA).
> NOBODY'S FAULT. (*See* KEYNOTES SERIES.)

TABB (JOHN B.).
POEMS. Sq. 32mo. 4s. 6d. net.
Boston: Copeland & Day.

TAYLOR (UNA).
NETS FOR THE WIND. (*See* KEYNOTES SERIES.)

TENNYSON (FREDERICK).
POEMS OF THE DAY AND YEAR. With a Title-page by
PATTEN WILSON. Crown 8vo. 5s. net.
Chicago: Stone & Kimball.

THIMM (C. A.).
A COMPLETE BIBLIOGRAPHY OF THE ART OF FENCE,
DUELLING, ETC. With Illustrations. [*In preparation.*

THOMPSON (FRANCIS).
POEMS. With Frontispiece, Title-page, and Cover Design
by LAURENCE HOUSMAN. Fourth Edition. Pott
4to. 5s. net.
Boston: Copeland & Day.
SISTER SONGS: An Offering to Two Sisters. With Frontis-
piece, Title-page, and Cover Design by LAURENCE
HOUSMAN. Pott 4to. 5s. net.
Boston: Copeland & Day.

THOREAU (HENRY DAVID).
POEMS OF NATURE. Selected and edited by HENRY S.
SALT and FRANK B. SANBORN, with a Title-page
designed by PATTEN WILSON. Fcap. 8vo. 4s. 6d.
net. [*In preparation.*
Boston and New York: Houghton, Mifflin & Co.

TYNAN HINKSON (KATHARINE).
CUCKOO SONGS. With Title-page and Cover Design by
LAURENCE HOUSMAN. Fcap. 8vo. 5s. net.
Boston: Copeland & Day.
MIRACLE PLAYS: OUR LORD'S COMING AND CHILDHOOD.
With Six Illustrations and a Title-page by PATTEN
WILSON. Fcap. 8vo. net. [*In preparation.*
Chicago: Stone & Kimball.

WATSON (ROSAMUND MARRIOTT).
VESPERTILIA AND OTHER POEMS. With a Title-page
designed by R. ANNING BELL. Fcap. 8vo. 4s. 6d.
net.
A SUMMER NIGHT AND OTHER POEMS. New edition,
with a decorative Title-page. Fcap. 8vo. 3s. net.
Chicago: Way & Williams. [*In preparation.*

WATSON (H. B. MARRIOTT).
AT THE FIRST CORNER. (*See* KEYNOTES SERIES.)
THE KING'S HIGHWAY. Crown 8vo. 4s. 6d. net.
[*In preparation.*

WATSON (WILLIAM).

ODES AND OTHER POEMS.    Fourth Edition.    Fcap. 8vo,
buckram.   4s. 6d. net.
New York : Macmillan & Co.

THE ELOPING ANGELS : A Caprice.    Second Edition.
Square 16mo, buckram.    3s. 6d. net.
New York : Macmillan & Co.

EXCURSIONS IN CRITICISM : being some Prose Recrea-
tions of a Rhymer.   Second Edition.   Cr. 8vo.   5s. net.
New York : Macmillan & Co.

THE PRINCE'S QUEST AND OTHER POEMS.    With a
Bibliographical Note added.    Second Edition.    Fcap.
8vo.   4s. 6d. net.

WATT (FRANCIS).

THE LAW'S LUMBER ROOM.   Fcap. 8vo.   3s. 6d. net.
Chicago : A. C. McClurg & Co.

WATTS (THEODORE).

POEMS.   Crown 8vo.   5s. net.            [*In preparation.*
*There will also be an* Edition de Luxe *of this volume printed at*
*the Kelmscott Press.*

WELLS (H. G.).

SELECT CONVERSATIONS WITH AN UNCLE.    (*See* MAY-
FAIR SET.)

WHARTON (H. T.).

SAPPHO.    Memoir, Text, Selected Renderings, and a
Literal Translation by HENRY THORNTON WHARTON.
With three Illustrations in Photogravure, and a Cover
designed   by   AUBREY   BEARDSLEY.    Fcap. 8vo.
7s. 6d. net.
Chicago : A. C. McClurg & Co.

# THE YELLOW BOOK

## An Illustrated Quarterly

*Pott 4to.   5s. net.*

VOLUME I.    April 1894.   272 pages.   15 Illustrations.
[*Out of print.*

VOLUME II.    July 1894.   364 pages.   23 Illustrations.
VOLUME III.   October 1894.   280 pages.   15 Illustrations.
VOLUME IV.   January 1895.   285 pages.   16 Illustrations.
VOLUME V.   April 1895.   317 pages.   14 Illustrations.
VOLUME VI.   July 1895.   335 pages.   16 Illustrations.
Boston : Copeland & Day.